OFF COURSE

ALSO BY GEORGINA BLOOMBERG
& CATHERINE HAPKA

The A Circuit
My Favorite Mistake

OFF COURSE

AN A CIRCUIT NOVEL

GEORGINA BLOOMBERG & CATHERINE HAPKA

BLOOMSBURY

NEW YORK LONDON NEW DELHI SYDNEY

To my amazing friends, who have stuck
with me through the good and the bad
—G. B.

First published in the United States of America in November 2012
by Bloomsbury Books for Young Readers
www.bloomsburyteens.com

For information about permission to reproduce selections from this book, write to
Permissions, Bloomsbury BFYR, 175 Fifth Avenue, New York, New York 10010

Library of Congress Cataloging-in-Publication Data
Bloomberg, Georgina.
Off course : an A circuit novel / by Georgina Bloomberg and Catherine Hapka.
        p.   cm.
Summary: Tommi, Kate, and Zara, teen equestrians on horseback riding's elite A circuit, should be
preparing for the biggest show of the season, but boyfriend problems, a road trip, and a gossip blog
interfere with their training.
ISBN 978-1-59990-909-7
[1. Horse shows—Fiction. 2. Horsemanship—Fiction. 3. Friendship—Fiction. 4. Wealth—Fiction.]
I. Hapka, Catherine. II. Title.
PZ7.B62345Of 2012   [Fic]—dc23   2012009587

Book design by Regina Roff
Typeset by Westchester Book Composition
Printed in the U.S.A. by Quad/Graphics, Fairfield, Pennsylvania
2 4 6 8 10 9 7 5 3 1

All papers used by Bloomsbury Publishing, Inc., are natural, recyclable products
made from wood grown in well-managed forests. The manufacturing processes
conform to the environmental regulations of the country of origin.

ONE

— — — — —

"What are you having? Want to split some fries?"

Kate blinked and glanced up from the menu. She'd been
staring at the words printed there without really seeing them.
Not that it mattered. She'd been to the diner so often she knew
the entire menu by heart. Still, she felt guilty as she realized
she had no idea what Fitz had been saying to her for the past
five minutes.

Fitz. Her boyfriend. Her rich, impulsive, adorably demented
boyfriend, the one who'd just dropped the world's biggest
bombshell on her. At least it felt that way.

"Um, it's still kind of early for fries, isn't it?" Kate said. "I
was thinking about having pancakes or something."

Maybe a nice big breakfast will get Tommi and Zara off my
back, she thought as she set her menu on the table.

She couldn't help a slight grimace as she thought about how
the two girls had ambushed her at the barn. Could they really
think she was on the verge of some terrible eating disorder

just because she'd been extra busy lately and dropped a few pounds? Sure, she could maybe see Zara thinking that way; she was still new to Pelham Lane Stables and didn't know Kate very well. Besides, Zara seemed like kind of a drama magnet herself. No wonder, with the life she had—rock-star dad, movie-star mom, all the money and attention she could possibly want.

But that didn't explain Tommi's reaction. She'd always been Kate's best friend at the barn. The two of them tended to see eye to eye on most subjects dealing with horses, riding, and training.

Was that enough to base a real friendship on, though? Maybe Kate had been too quick to forget that she and Tommi had about as much in common as a sleek imported warmblood and a scruffy little Chincoteague pony. Tommi's privileged Manhattan lifestyle was as far as it got from the blue-collar small town where Kate had grown up.

Thinking about her hometown reminded Kate of another friend, one she had a lot more in common with—Nat. And that brought her thudding back to the here and now. She really needed to figure out how she was going to handle this latest potential disaster.

Luckily Fitz hadn't noticed her expression—he'd just turned away to signal to the nearest waitress. "Never too early for fries." He grinned, snapping his menu shut. "I'll order 'em, and you can pick if you want, okay?"

"Sure, sounds good."

After they'd placed their orders, Fitz leaned back against the faded vinyl seat of their booth, stretching his long, lean arms over his head.

"Anyway, back to Flame," he said. "Were you surprised? I really wanted it to be a surprise."

Kate pasted a smile on her face, hoping it looked genuine. "Yeah," she said. "I was definitely surprised."

That was the understatement of the century. Okay, so she was getting used to Fitz's impulsive behavior. Sort of, anyway. But she'd never expected him to do something like *this*.

"I still can't believe you actually bought him," she said. "Especially right now, when your parents and Jamie are still mad at you."

Fitz looked pleased with himself. "You're psyched, though, right?"

Kate wasn't sure what to say. Yes, she'd liked the tall chestnut gelding Nat had been riding at the little local show. She'd liked him a lot, actually. Flame was fresh off the racetrack, a little scruffy and confused about his new job as a lesson horse, but his quality and good temperament had stood out despite all that. Still, Kate had never imagined Fitz would decide to actually *buy* the horse based on her comments. Who *did* stuff like that?

Luckily Fitz didn't wait for her to answer before continuing. "I mean, I know Flame doesn't exactly fit in at Pelham Lane right now," he said. "But Jamie had the same reaction you did when he first saw him."

"Really?"

"Uh-huh." Fitz gulped down half the water in his glass, then wiped his lips with the back of one hand. "Said he was a real diamond in the rough. I tried to pretend I found him myself, but Jamie knew right away you must've had something to do with it." He shrugged. "He said you've always been great at seeing a horse's potential."

Kate felt her face flush slightly. Jamie Vos, the owner and head trainer of Pelham Lane Stables, didn't hand out compliments like that very often. Had he really said it, or was Fitz exaggerating as usual? "If that's true, it's only because Jamie taught me everything I know," she mumbled.

"Not everything." Fitz leaned across the table and brushed back a strand of hair that had drifted loose from her ponytail. "And I should know. I may be hopeless when it comes to horseflesh, but I've got a great eye for a beautiful girl."

"Yeah, that's what they say," Kate joked weakly, though she couldn't help shivering as his fingers, still cold from the icy water glass, grazed her skin. Would she ever get used to having him look at her that way?

Fitz grinned. "Anyway, the A circuit won't know what hit them once the great Kate Nilsen enters the ring with her new superstar. You'll see!"

"You mean *your* new superstar," Kate corrected.

"Whatever." Fitz shrugged. "I wouldn't have him if you hadn't let me tag along to that schooling show. I figure that makes him at least half yours, right?"

After that, Fitz chattered on for a while about his plans for the new horse, barely pausing when the waitress dropped their food on the table. But Kate hardly heard a word he said. Now that the shock was wearing off, her mind couldn't stop skimming over the facts of what was happening here, poking at them like a tongue seeking out a sore tooth. Trying to figure out how this was going to turn out okay, or at least not blow up into a total disaster.

I wonder if Nat knows yet? she thought. Flame was

supposed to be her big training project. She was going to have an aneurysm when she found out he was at Pelham Lane now—and that it was all Kate's fault.

Kate felt her fingers clench around her fork. Glancing down, she realized she'd cut one of her pancakes into almost a dozen pieces and was now sliding one of those pieces around and around, leaving smeary little trails in the syrup. Oops. How long had she been sitting there, not eating? She quickly raised the fork, but paused with the dripping bit of pancake suspended a few inches from her mouth. The sickly sweet smell of the syrup made her stomach shudder.

Fitz glanced up from his half-eaten burger. "Your pancakes okay?" he asked. "If you changed your mind about the breakfast thing, there's still time to order a sandwich or something instead."

"No, I'm good." Kate shoved the fork into her mouth, not giving herself a chance to overthink it. The pancake felt heavy on her tongue, and she almost gagged as she forced herself to start chewing.

But once she swallowed the first bite, her stomach growled for more. She was ravenous, and no wonder. When had she last eaten more than a few bites of something out of the vending machine? She was going to have to be more careful about that.

She was scooping up the last piece of soggy pancake when she saw Fitz signal for the waitress again. "Don't tell me you're ordering another burger," she said, surveying his tall, lanky frame. "I don't know where you put all that food you eat!"

"Hollow leg. Medically documented." He leaned over and

slid one finger through the leftover syrup on her plate, then licked it off. "No, actually I've got to jet. I'm supposed to meet my folks back in the city for lunch, remember? I told you earlier. They're leaving tonight for Copenhagen, and I promised I'd be there for the bon voyage lunch."

"Copenhagen?" Kate echoed blankly.

"Yeah. It's August. Time for the annual Hall family European vacation." Fitz wiped his sticky finger on his napkin and then pulled out his wallet, flipping through several credit cards before selecting one and dropping it atop the check the waitress had left them. "Since I'm still in the doghouse, I probably shouldn't ditch this lunch. Though after everything that's happened this summer, I'm kind of surprised they still want to see me at all. Go figure, right?"

Kate shook her head, her brain feeling as sticky and slow as the syrup congealing on her plate. "Wait," she said. "Didn't you go with them on that trip last year? I remember you missed the Washington Crossing show and a couple of others."

He reached over and tweaked her chin playfully. "So you *were* paying attention to me even way back then," he joked. "And here I thought you only had eyes for the horses!"

"Very funny." Kate rolled her eyes. "But seriously, why aren't you going with?"

"Why would I want to spend the whole month on another continent when I could be here with you? I couldn't survive being away from you that long."

Kate wasn't sure what to say to that. Was that really why Fitz was sticking around instead of jetting off to Europe with his wealthy parents?

Or is it because he's not invited this year? she wondered with a pang of guilt. *Maybe they're still mad at him for the Ford thing.*

She still felt tense every time she thought about that. At a show earlier in the season, Zara had crashed one of Jamie's sale horses during a drunken joyride. She'd been ready to confess, even though it meant she'd be kicked out of the barn for sure. When Fitz had noticed that Kate was upset about that he'd stepped forward, taking the blame in Zara's place.

Most people still didn't really understand why he'd done it. But Kate did. It was his warped, Fitz-like way of apologizing for something that had happened between them—well, *almost* happened—in the hay stall that same evening. His version of a big, dramatic gesture, a way to prove how much he cared, how sorry he was for pushing her too hard.

In any case, Kate reminded herself that she hadn't asked him to do any of that. He was a big boy, and could make his own decisions. Whatever his reasons for skipping the European vacation, she wasn't going to worry about it.

No, she had plenty of other things to worry about right now.

Kate yawned as she climbed out of her car and headed up the front walk to her house. The crickets were humming, the stifling heat of the summer afternoon was finally fading with the last of the daylight, and somewhere down the block a dog barked hoarsely in someone's backyard.

It had been a long day. The barn was technically closed on

Mondays, which meant there were no lessons, no training rides, and virtually no customers around. But horses required care 24/7/365, and the only way Kate could afford to ride at a top show barn like Pelham Lane was by working there.

Glancing at her watch, Kate wondered if she should try calling Nat. Maybe it would be better if she heard the news from the horse's mouth, so to speak.

Reaching into her pocket, she touched her phone, trying to imagine how the conversation might go. *Hi, Nat? It's your so-called BFF, Kate. Guess what? My rich boyfriend just bought the horse you're crazy about out from under you because I told him it was pretty. Surprise!*

She winced, wishing she'd never agreed to go to that schooling show at her old lesson barn. Or at least that she hadn't let Fitz invite himself along. Then he never would've seen Flame, and her life would be a lot less complicated right now . . .

As she reached the front door, she heard muffled shouting from inside. Uh-oh. It sounded like her father and younger brother were yelling at each other again. That was nothing unusual these days. Andy and his new loser friends seemed to spend most of their time looking for trouble—and usually finding it. As a cop, Kate's father didn't have much patience for that sort of behavior, and he wasn't afraid to let Andy know that.

Kate opened the door and slipped inside, planning to hurry upstairs before she could get caught up in the family drama. But she stopped short when she saw two uniformed officers flanking her father in the front room. All three men were glaring at Andy, who stood slouched and hands-in-pocket against the far wall. Kate's mother was huddled on the couch nearby, sobbing quietly into a wadded-up paper towel.

Kate's father glanced over. "Katie," he said in his gruff-cop voice. "You're home."

"Um, hi," she said. "What's going on?"

She shifted her gaze to Andy, who stared back defiantly. "It's no big deal," he muttered. "Anyway, I didn't do it."

"Do what?" Kate asked, even though she wasn't sure she wanted to know the answer.

"Andy's math teacher had his house tagged and his car vandalized earlier this evening," her father replied grimly. "And we're pretty sure Andy and that new gang of thugs he hangs out with had something to do with it."

"Excuse me, Miss Trask. What would you like us to do with this?"

Zara looked up, squinting against the morning sun glaring in through the loft's huge bank of windows. One of the cleaning crew guys was standing there, holding up several pieces of what had once been a large glass vase. The guy was kind of cute in an outer-boroughs kind of way, but she didn't dwell on that. This wasn't the time.

"Not worth trying to fix that ugly thing," she said, stifling a yawn. She'd been up since six—a decent enough hour to go to bed, but a seriously sucky time to wake up. "Go ahead and chuck it."

The guy hurried off, and Zara returned her attention to the wad of dried chewing gum she was trying to scrape off the coffee table with a butter knife. Cleaning wasn't her favorite way to spend a sunny summer Tuesday morning. Or any other time, actually. But she didn't have much choice, thanks to Cousin Stacie.

Cousin Stacie. Every time she thought about her, Zara's blood pressure spiked. Even after all that had happened, she still couldn't believe the girl had just taken off, skipped town with no warning. How ridiculous was it to feel abandoned when Zara hadn't even wanted her around in the first place?

Before she could figure that out, her cell phone buzzed. "Hopefully it's Mom saying she missed her flight," Zara muttered under her breath.

But when she glanced at the screen, she sighed. Definitely not her mother. It was a text from Grant.

hey, sexy, the text read. *what u up to? want to get together soon? I miss u!*

Zara tossed the phone back on the sleek retro-modern sofa without responding. She wasn't in the mood to deal with Grant right now.

She heard the clink of breaking glass and glanced that way. The worker had just tossed the vase pieces into the big plastic bin they were using to haul trash down to their truck. Now he was brushing off his hands and staring at the framed gold and platinum records arrayed artfully on one wall. Was he a Zac Trask fan, or just curious? Zara didn't know and cared even less. She just wanted the loft clean already.

It was getting there, but not fast enough. A couple of guys were busy sanding puke stains off the hardwood, other workers were polishing, sweeping, and scrubbing various surfaces, and a bossy-looking woman was wiping smudges off the plasma TV. Zara knew the woman was the foreman of the work crew, though she couldn't remember her name. Wendy, Wanda? Something like that.

"How much longer is this going to take?" Zara called out, hurrying toward her.

"It's coming along, Miss Trask," Wendy-Wanda-Whatever said, her voice and smile way too perky and energetic for someone who cleaned up other people's messes for a living. "The kitchen and bathrooms are spotless, and they're just finishing up in the bedrooms, so we'll be focused on taking care of things in here now."

Zara bit her lip, scanning the enormous main room. Her mother's charter flight from Vancouver was scheduled to land any minute. There was no way Zara could let her find the cleaning crew, or she would know something was up. But she also couldn't chase them out early—it was still way too obvious that there had been some serious partying going on in here.

Obvious answer? Make sure her mother didn't come home for a while. But how?

"Lunch," Zara murmured, realizing it was almost noon. She grabbed her phone again, staring at it. She could text her mother and suggest meeting somewhere for a welcome-home lunch.

The trouble was, if Zara suggested a place here in SoHo, her mother would definitely want to stop in at the loft and touch up her face first. It wouldn't do for a big-time movie star like Gina Girard to be seen looking less than glammo-perfect at all times.

No, Zara had to keep her out of the neighborhood. She wandered over to the bar and studied the framed map of New York City hanging behind it. It was a stylized collage-type thing done by some lame-ass modern art guy her mom had met at one of her film premieres, but it still showed most of the basics. Zara quickly located JFK Airport, then traced the route into Manhattan with her finger.

"Midtown," she murmured. "East side, right on the way in. That should work."

She hurried out to the entry alcove and dug through the messy stack of phone books and takeout menus on the countertop until she found the Zagat guide, which listed restaurants all over the city. Flipping it open to a random page, Zara scanned for Midtown addresses. The first one she spotted looked like a burger joint—not exactly her mother's style—but then she saw another listing just below it, this one for a place she'd never heard of called La Vache Folle.

"French," Zara muttered. "She'll love that."

She scanned the entry, which mostly involved terms like "delish rustic fare" and "charmingly quirky." Good enough. She quickly texted her mother, suggesting the two of them meet up there. Okay, so they didn't have a reservation, but Zara wasn't worried about that. Gina's famous face would get them in. It always did.

"Gotta go," she told the foreman. "You guys need to be done and cleared out of here in like two hours max, okay?"

"We'll do our best," the woman replied.

"Do better than that." Zara grabbed her purse and headed for the door, then paused and turned back as a thought occurred to her. "Actually, though, don't make it look *too* perfect, okay? Leave my shoes out in the main room, maybe a couple of glasses in the drying rack by the sink, some magazines lying around. Stuff like that. You know—so the place looks lived in."

Wendy-Wanda raised an eyebrow, then nodded and smiled as Zara pulled a fifty out of her purse and handed it over. "Whatever you say," the foreman said. "You're the boss."

Good. That was one big problem taken care of. Now Zara just had one more.

What was she supposed to say when Gina noticed that Cousin Stacie wasn't around?

"Oh, Miss Tommi. Sorry, dear, I thought you'd already left for the barn."

Tommi glanced up from her makeup mirror. Mrs. Grigoryan had just bustled into her room with an armful of clean laundry.

"I'm leaving soon," Tommi told the housekeeper, capping her mascara. "Have you seen my boots?"

"Downstairs front closet."

"Thanks."

Mrs. Grigoryan dropped the clothes on a chair and left. Tommi was pulling her straight brown hair into a ponytail when she heard her phone buzz. Less than ten seconds later, it buzzed again.

She was tempted to ignore the texts and catch up later. The juniors' weekly group lesson wasn't until that afternoon, but

Tommi had a lot to do before then. She'd been so busy with her current sales project, an imported jumper gelding named Legs, that she hadn't been spending as much time as usual with her other horses. They were all impeccably trained, experienced show horses, but they weren't robots. At this past show, Tommi had noticed that her hunter, Toccata, had been extra spooky and fresh off the leg, while her junior jumper was a little sluggish in the jump-off. She was planning to hack both of them and then spend a few minutes lungeing her eq horse before it was time to get Legs ready for the lesson.

But she couldn't resist checking on the new texts. She smiled when she saw who had sent the first one.

"Alex," she murmured to herself, flashing back to Sunday evening. He'd been waiting at her house when she arrived home from last week's show. The two of them had grabbed some dinner, then ended up staying out at this little hole-in-the-wall place in the West Village listening to Alex's friends' reggae fusion band until Tommi was too tired to keep her eyes open.

hey, the text read, *just got some cool news. got called in to sub for the regular DJ at that new club on the lower east side I was telling u about. Gig is Wed. night. Wanna come cheer me on?*

Tommi was about to text him back to say she'd be there. Then she remembered that second buzz and clicked to the next text, wanting to make sure it wasn't Alex texting back to correct the date or something.

But the second message was from her friend Brooke.

Yo Aaronson! Up for a road trip? Moving in early at Penn

and could use some moral support from my girls. Leaving Fri a.m. & spending the weekend at my cousin's place (aka party central). Wanna come?

Tommi glanced at the calendar on her desk, though she didn't need to—she had Pelham Lane's show schedule memorized. She already knew that the barn was taking next weekend off to prepare for one of Tommi's favorite shows of the entire year, the prestigious Washington Crossing charity show, which took place on the grounds of a picturesque historic estate down in Bucks County, Pennsylvania.

That meant there was no reason she couldn't go on the road trip. It would be good to spend some quality time with Brooke before she left for college. The two of them had barely seen each other all summer, thanks to Tommi's riding and Brooke's internship at the *Times*. Besides that, Tommi could guess who the other "girls" involved were—Court and Abby for sure, probably Jordan, maybe Mariah. All of them a guaranteed blast. As a bonus, she knew her father would be thrilled if she told him she wanted to spend the weekend visiting a university campus, even if it wasn't his beloved Georgetown. And now that they were business partners, sort of, she was all about keeping him happy.

Still, she hesitated, thumbs poised over her phone's keypad. Thinking about Brooke starting college reminded her that summer was on its way out. Her own senior year would be gearing up again in a matter of weeks, and part of the deal with her father was that she had to get Legs sold by the last of the big fall shows. That was how she was supposed to start proving to him that she could actually make a career out of horses. Did she really have time to goof off for a whole weekend right now?

Deciding to think about it later, she quickly typed *sounds fun, but not sure yet, let me check my sched & get back to u.*

She stuck the phone in her pocket and hurried downstairs to find her boots.

TWO

— — — — —

Kate maneuvered the mower into its spot in the equipment shed and cut the engine. She sat there for a moment, breathing in the smells of gasoline and grass clippings, trying to remember what she was supposed to do next.

"Clean out the grain bin," she murmured finally, wiping her sweaty forehead on the hem of her T-shirt. "Or wait—did I do that already?"

She climbed down from the mower with a weary sigh. She'd been in a fog all morning. Her dad's two cop buddies hadn't left her house until almost 1:00 a.m. last night, after plenty of yelling and drama. The good news was that they hadn't actually arrested Andy. Probably only because he was police family, though Kate wasn't sure how much longer that would help him—their dad was furious, and it didn't help that Andy was acting sullen and ungrateful about being let off the hook. The whole situation was such a mess that it had almost distracted Kate from worrying about Nat and Flame.

Almost.

She hurried into the main barn, pausing when she saw Flame hanging his head out over his stall guard, his forelock and mane blowing around in the breeze of the fan tied to the grill of his stall. In spite of everything, Kate couldn't help smiling as she noted the way his delicate ears almost touched at the tips when he pointed them toward her, his big soft eyes watching as she came closer.

"Hey, boy," she whispered, stepping over to give him a pat. "How you doing?"

The horse snuffled at her as Kate ran a hand down his long, arched neck, admiring the clean way it tied in to his withers. Yes, she'd been right about this guy—he was a looker, and built to perform, too. So wasn't it better that he was in a place where he could live up to his potential? Jamie seemed to think so, and so did Fitz. Kate suspected Nat might not agree.

Once again, she wondered if she should call Nat and at least try to head off the coming disaster somehow. Checking her watch, she saw that she had almost an hour before she needed to start tacking up for the group lesson. But what would she say? Nat wasn't the most reasonable, coolheaded, or logical person in the world. Maybe it would be better to talk to her face-to-face. Then again, maybe not.

"Never mind," she whispered to Flame, who was nuzzling curiously at her shirt as she rubbed his neck. "I've got too much to do to worry about it right now."

She gave the horse one last pat and turned away, ready to get back to work. To her surprise, she saw Fitz coming down the aisle.

"Not only beautiful, but a mind reader, too." He greeted her with a grin, planting a kiss on top of her head.

"Huh?" She was a little distracted, as always, by having him so close. He smelled good—spicy and earthy, like aftershave and fresh hay. Kate couldn't help feeling self-conscious about her own smell, which couldn't be nearly as pleasant after a morning spent slogging through chores in the muggy August weather.

"I thought maybe we could take Flame for a quick spin," Fitz said, reaching past her to pat the chestnut gelding. "Traffic sucked getting out here, but we've still got some time before lessons."

"Oh." Kate glanced over her shoulder at Flame. "Um, are you sure that's a good idea? He just got here, and Nat said he's only been off the track a couple of weeks. It might be better to give him more time to settle in and get used to things."

"I'm not saying we should make him jump a Grand Prix course or anything. Just get him out and see what our new boy can really do."

Fitz shot her his crooked, slightly wicked grin, the one that made her melt a little inside every time it was aimed her way. The one that could get her to do almost anything he asked. But this time Kate knew she shouldn't give in.

"I've got a better idea," she said. "Flame could definitely use a little TLC to make him look like he fits in at Pelham Lane. How about we do a spa day instead?"

For a second Fitz looked unconvinced. Then he shrugged and grinned again. "Sounds kind of girly, but I'm in. I'll go grab the clippers and stuff and meet you in the grooming stall."

Soon the two of them were fussing over the horse. The grooms had bathed him upon arrival, but there was still a lot to do before he was turned out to Pelham Lane's exacting standards. Fitz had also brought out his iPod, plugging it into a pair of portable speakers. He started singing along with the songs as he worked, acting out the lyrics or just dancing around with his long limbs flying.

Kate's mind was still churning with worries about Nat, her family, and everything else. But Fitz's mood was infectious, and before long she caught herself having a good time. She could tell that Flame was enjoying the pampering session, too. He didn't object when she trimmed his whiskers or pulled his mane, though he kept trying to nibble on the pulling comb.

"He's really a nice boy, isn't he?" Kate murmured, mostly to herself, fighting back a wave of guilt as she tried not to imagine what Nat would say if she could see them right now.

Fitz heard her and glanced over. "You definitely know how to pick them," he said with a wink. Then his eyes lit up as a new song came on the iPod. "Ooh, love this tune! Dance with me?"

He grabbed Kate by the wrist and twirled her toward him, making her drop the clippers. She laughed, almost tripping over the power cord as he pressed her against him.

"Stop," she protested, suddenly feeling a little breathless. "I work here, remember? I can't get away with goofing off in public like you can."

"Relax. Nobody'll blame you. Everyone already knows I'm a bad influence." He shot her that wicked grin again, then chucked her chin up with one finger and kissed her.

Kate went with it, trying to let all the stresses of the past few weeks disappear as she kissed him back. But when Flame let out a sudden snort and shifted his weight, she pulled away.

"Enough," she said as sternly as she could manage. "We're going to embarrass Flame with all the PDA."

"He'll get over it." Fitz reached out, trying to pull her back in. But Kate twisted away, then grabbed a bottle of coat conditioner off the wire rack on the wall behind her and squirted it at him. She giggled and ducked as he let out a howl of surprise and lunged at her.

"No fair!" he exclaimed. "You'll pay for that!"

Kate laughed again, then ducked under Flame's neck and scooted around him, trying to keep the horse's body between herself and Fitz. Flame pricked his ears but remained relaxed, one hind foot cocked as he watched them chase each other around.

Finally Kate stopped and held up both hands. "I surrender!" she said breathlessly, wiping a few beads of sweat off her forehead. Even with the fans going, it was hot in the barn. "If I give you one more kiss, will you behave yourself and let us get back to work?"

Fitz stroked his chin with one hand, pretending to mull it over. "Is that your best offer?" he joked. Then he reached for her. "Come here, you."

Kate lost track of time a little bit as they kissed again. When Fitz finally came up for air, she felt dizzy. "Okay," she said, doing her best to shake it off. "Back to work. I'll finish doing his ears if you work on his tail."

"Deal."

A few minutes later, Kate was unplugging the clippers

when Flame lifted his head, pricking his ears at someone coming down the aisle. Kate glanced over her shoulder and saw Summer Campbell coming toward them. Summer was scheduled to ride in the juniors' group lesson in a little while, though she was only half dressed for it right now in breeches and a pair of expensive-looking beaded flip-flops.

"Fitz! There you are!" she exclaimed.

Fitz lifted one hand in a lazy wave. "Yo, Summer. What's up?"

"Careful," Kate added as Summer ducked under Flame's head to get to Fitz. "You don't want Flame to step on your foot while you're wearing those shoes."

"What? Oh, hi, I didn't see you." Summer barely glanced at Kate before turning her attention back to Fitz. "So listen," she said. "You'll never believe my big news."

"Really? What is it?" Fitz spritzed Flame's tail with conditioner.

Summer smiled, tossing her long, straight blond hair back over one shoulder—a move that should have looked casual and natural but somehow, coming from Summer, seemed as artificial and trying-too-hard as the blingy Swarovski crystals that studded the belt she was wearing. "Ah, ah, ah!" She waggled a finger in Fitz's face. "It's a secret. But if you're all nice to me, I just might make a big announcement during today's group lesson."

"Sure you don't want to give us a preview?" Fitz said with a grin. "We can keep a secret. Right, Kate?"

"Um . . . ," Kate began.

Summer didn't bother to wait for her to respond. "Sorry,

guys," she singsonged playfully. "You're just going to have to wait like everyone else. See you in the lesson!"

She rushed off down the aisle. Fitz watched her go, one eyebrow raised.

"Wonder what that's all about?" he commented.

Kate shrugged. She had more important things to worry about than the latest drama in Summer's happy little world. "Come on," she said, picking up a grooming mitt. "We'd better finish up here before it's time to tack up."

"Good boy." Tommi gave her eq horse, a massive dark bay Hanoverian named Orion, a pat on his damp neck. "Bet that felt good, didn't it?"

She'd just finished hosing the horse down after his workout. Checking her watch, she saw that she only had a few minutes until she needed to start warming up for the group lesson. It was a good thing she'd asked one of the grooms to get Legs ready for her, because she still had one more thing to do.

As she left Orion in his stall, she heard a sudden shout of laughter. Fitz. Okay, that made things easier. Wherever he was these days, Kate was likely to be there, too.

Tommi still wasn't sure what to think about that. Fitz had been working his way through the girls of the A circuit pretty much since hitting puberty. Tommi knew she hadn't been the only one taken by surprise when he'd fallen hard for Kate earlier that summer. She just hoped Fitz was as serious about her friend as he seemed. Kate didn't have much experience with guys, and Tommi didn't want to see her get hurt.

Rounding the corner, she saw the two of them in the grooming stall fussing over that rangy Thoroughbred Fitz had just bought. The horse still looked thin, but now his ears and muzzle were freshly trimmed, his mane was pulled and conditioned, and his white socks and blaze gleamed against his coppery coat.

"Hey," Tommi said as she approached. "He's looking good."

"Thanks." Kate reached up to give the horse a scratch on the withers, which made him stretch his neck out and flop his lower lip with pleasure. "He's a nice boy—I think he likes being pampered."

"Who wouldn't like having *you* pampering him, gorgeous?" Fitz told her with that cocky little smile that all the girls seemed to find so irresistible. Well, all the girls except Tommi, anyway. Somehow she'd always been immune to his particular set of charms, though she liked him well enough as a friend.

There was a clatter of hooves at the end of the aisle. Tommi glanced up just in time to see one of the other juniors, Dani, walking past with a horse trailing behind her.

Fitz saw her, too. "Oops—looks like people are starting to get ready."

"You'd better go tack up," Tommi told him. "You're not exactly on Jamie's top ten list of favorite people right now, in case you forgot."

"You have a point." Fitz glanced across the chestnut gelding's back at Kate. "Can you put this guy away? I don't even know where my boots are right now, and last time I saw Chip he had a huge manure stain on his butt."

Kate nodded. "I've got it. Go ahead."

"Thanks, beautiful." Fitz blew her a kiss. "See you guys in the ring." He grabbed his iPod and loped off.

"I should get ready, too." Kate unclipped Flame from the crossties. "Fitz's horse isn't the only one that's dirty. Fable looks like he spent the entire night of turnout rolling in the mud."

"That's a gray horse for you. I'll help you get him cleaned up." Tommi fell into step as Kate led Flame down the aisle. "Max is tacking up Legs for me. And I wanted to talk to you."

"Oh?" Kate shot her a cautious look. "Um, that's good, because I actually kind of wanted to talk to you, too."

Tommi was a little surprised, though she tried not to show it. Kate wasn't exactly famous for opening up to people. "Okay, well, here I am," she said. "Let's talk."

They'd reached Flame's stall by then. Kate fell silent as she led the gelding in and removed his halter. She stepped out and fastened the stall guard, then turned to face Tommi, twisting the halter's leather crownpiece in both hands.

"I just wanted to say, um, you know, I appreciate it," she said in a voice so quiet that Tommi had to lean closer to hear it. "You know. Trying to help me. At the show with the breeches, then afterward with Zara . . ."

Tommi nodded. At the last show, Kate had accidentally ruined her only show-ring-worthy pair of breeches. No biggie, it could happen to anyone—which was why Tommi didn't understand why Kate hadn't just come to her right away. Or to Jamie, for that matter, or any of half a dozen others who would have been happy to help. Instead Kate had slipped a new pair of breeches onto the tab of a wealthy adult client without telling her. She'd had second thoughts almost immediately, but before she could return the breeches she'd fallen off a horse and ruined them. Only then had she finally confided in Tommi, who'd helped smooth things over so that no one else would ever need to know what Kate had done.

"Anytime," Tommi told Kate now. "And I'm sorry if I was out of line, coming at you with Zara like that. We just—"

"No, it's okay," Kate interrupted, her cheeks going pink. "I mean, I guess I can't blame you guys for being worried, considering what happened—you know, me passing out in the middle of a course like that. That's not exactly normal behavior." She rolled her eyes and sighed. "I've been so busy lately that maybe I haven't scheduled in enough time for stuff like eating and sleeping. And with all the extra stress at home—"

"What's going on at home?" Tommi asked cautiously. Kate didn't talk about her home life much. Tommi had never even been inside her house, though she'd dropped her off at the curb a few times.

Kate turned to scratch Flame's cheek as he stuck his head out and nuzzled her. She was quiet for so long that Tommi was afraid she wasn't going to answer at all.

But finally she spoke. "It's my brother," she said, running her hand down Flame's long, white-splashed nose. "He's turning into some kind of juvenile delinquent. Just got accused of trashing one of his teacher's houses over the weekend."

"Whoa." Tommi shook her head. "That sounds like bad news. No wonder you're extra stressed lately. But listen, you can't let it get to you so much, okay? I don't ever want to see you come off a horse like that again." She shuddered as she flashed back to Kate passing out right after an extra-big jump and flopping to the ground like an old rag doll.

"I know." Kate's voice went quiet again. "I'm sorry."

"Don't be sorry. Just let me help you make it better, okay?"

"Yeah." Kate shrugged. "I mean, I'm pretty sure I don't really have a problem. Not the kind you and Zara were talking about, anyway. I just got kind of, you know, distracted, I guess. No big deal."

Tommi hoped she was right. "Okay," she said. "Let's go with that for now. But I'm not going to take any chances, got it? I want to know you're eating enough from now on. And if I even think you're not, I'll have to talk to Jamie or your parents or somebody."

"You won't have to do that," Kate said quickly. She paused, still stroking Flame's face. "But if you wanted to, like, help remind me to eat when I get busy, that would be good. I think it might help."

"Deal. I'll start now." Tommi smiled. "What did you have for lunch today?"

"Um . . ."

"That's what I thought." Tommi fished in the pocket of her jeans, pulling out a granola bar. She'd grabbed it on the way out of the house, planning to eat it on the long drive up to West-chester County. But she'd ended up hitting the drive-through at a bagel shop instead, so there it was, slightly squashed but still edible. "Here—eat this, and then let's go get Fable ready."

Summer glanced up as Tommi rode into the ring a short while later. "Hey!" she called out. "Have you seen Zara today?"

Tommi glanced at her, still distracted by her talk with Kate earlier. Kate had eaten the entire granola bar, which made Tommi feel better. Maybe she was right—maybe all she needed was a friend looking out for her. She hoped so. Kate could be pretty intense. Sometimes that was good, like when she channeled it into her riding or grooming or whatever. But Tommi was starting to realize there was a dark side to it, too.

"Um, what?" she said, realizing Summer was staring at her.

"Zara." Summer sounded impatient. "Have you seen her? She's not here yet, and Joy said she didn't call to cancel."

"What, are you stalking her or something?" Tommi was surprised that Summer hadn't given up on becoming BFFs with Zara yet. It wasn't as if Zara had ever given her much encouragement. Then again, Summer was probably the shallowest person Tommi had ever met, as obsessed with wealth, fame, and status as her new-money parents. Befriending someone like Zara was probably like her Holy Grail. "Anyway, I haven't seen her either," Tommi added.

Summer rode off toward Marissa and Dani, who were walking their horses side by side at the other end of the ring. Tommi halted Legs and bent forward to double-check her girth.

"I hope Zara's not late again." Kate rode up next to her. "Jamie's not going to be happy if she is."

Tommi nodded, letting Legs walk on. "She seemed awfully distracted yesterday. Kept blabbing the whole drive out here about her cousin disappearing or whatever."

"Her cousin? What do you mean?" Kate half-halted Fable as he skittered sideways, snorting at a blowing leaf.

Fable, whose full name was Fabelhaften, was one of Jamie's sales horses. He'd already had careers as a pretty good dressage horse and a mediocre show hunter, but Jamie thought the beefy gray warmblood was best suited as an equitation horse. He'd asked Kate to start riding him in the hypercompetitive 3'6" Big Eq classes, and while Kate seemed surprised and a little overwhelmed by the offer, Tommi figured it was about time her friend got to show her stuff in the eq ring. So far the pair had been doing pretty well together. Sure, Fable could be a little goofy and sometimes liked to throw his considerable weight around—that was why he wasn't ready to go up for sale at Big Eq prices just yet. A quiet, tactful, patient rider like Kate was exactly what he needed to bring out his best and teach him his new job. Win-win.

Tommi waited until Kate had the big gray horse settled, then answered her question. "Zara's dad's on tour in Europe this summer, remember? And her mom's shooting a movie somewhere on the West Coast. So they got some distant cousin to come stay with Zara for the rest of the summer and keep an eye on her. I guess the cousin's a college student somewhere and wants to work in New York when she graduates."

"Oh." Kate still looked confused.

Tommi shook her head and smiled. Everything about Zara's life was the subject of major gossip at the barn. Leave it to Kate to be completely clueless!

"Anyway, the cousin turned out to be a total party hound," she explained. "So while Zara was away at the show last weekend, her cousin took off with some guy she met and left the place a total wreck—right when Zara found out her mom was about to pop home for a visit. Last I heard she was trying to hire a cleaning service to help her get it back in shape before her mom got there."

"Wow." Kate shook her head. "With all that going on, maybe she just forgot about today's lesson."

"Maybe. I'd better text her just in case."

Tommi let Legs walk out long and low along the rail as she quickly texted Zara a reminder. Then she picked up the reins and sent him into a trot, putting Zara's problems out of her mind as she started her warm-up.

Zara was still a no-show by the time Jamie strode into the ring, looking as dapper as ever in breeches, tall boots, and a hunter green polo with the barn's logo embroidered on it. "Everybody here?" the trainer said, glancing around at the riders as they brought their horses to a stop in a crooked line in front of him. "Where's Zara?"

"We don't know," Summer called out. "I mean, I'm sure she would have let me know if she wasn't coming. She's probably just running late."

Jamie frowned. Tommi winced, quickly checking her phone to see if Zara had texted her back. No new messages.

"Well, she'll have to catch up on her own if she bothers to show up," Jamie said, turning to adjust the jump behind him. "Pick up a trot, please. We'll do a little flatwork today before we move on to jumping. The Washington Crossing show is coming up soon, and I've noticed a few bad habits sneaking in for some of you over the past few shows . . ."

The lesson continued from there. Legs was full of energy, wanting to canter during the trot portions of their flatwork and gallop during the canter parts. But he listened to Tommi's aids, doing what she asked even when he felt ready to explode beneath her.

Once they turned to jumping, Legs overjumped the first few fences but then settled into the work, channeling his energy into the challenge of finding his way to the other side of the obstacles. He felt good, and Tommi found herself grinning at his sheer joy in doing his job. There had been many times she'd doubted her big idea to buy him as a resale project, many moments when she'd wondered if she was crazy to think she could make a go of it in the horse business. But times like this? Those worries were the furthest thing from her mind.

"Good boy!" Tommi exclaimed, giving him a pat as he landed after the final fence of the practice course Jamie had set up. Legs flagged his tail and sped up, tossing his head, and Tommi laughed.

"Nicely done," Jamie said as she brought the horse back to a trot and circled around to rejoin the group. "He's really improving."

"Thanks." Tommi patted her horse again. "I'm hoping he does well at Washington Crossing."

Jamie nodded, but his gaze had already moved on. "Dani, you're up next," he called out. "Really focus on keeping your body still when he takes off—I can tell that it bothers him when you jump ahead, and that's costing you rails in the show ring."

"Got it." Dani nodded, looking focused and determined as she gathered up her reins and sent her horse, a spunky Thoroughbred jumper known around the barn as Red, into a brisk canter.

Tommi's thoughts drifted as Dani started the course. Washington Crossing wasn't just another show for her and Legs. Getting him out and seen there could be a big step toward meeting her deadline, as long as—

She lost her train of thought when she heard a couple of the other students gasp. "Yikes," Kate said, her gaze trained on Dani.

Tommi tuned back in, realizing that Dani had flubbed the distance to the big oxer near the end of the course. Red had landed disorganized and strung out, his canter rushed and unbalanced as he headed for the last fence.

"Easy," Tommi murmured under her breath as she watched.

She could hear Dani talking to her horse, trying to regain his attention as he plunged toward the large vertical. At the same time Dani was tugging on the reins, obviously trying to get Red to put in another step. But he ignored her, launching himself from an impossibly long spot.

Tommi held her breath, willing the athletic horse to find a way over despite the bad takeoff. One front hoof cleared the top rail but the other smacked into it, followed by both hind legs. The jump collapsed with a clatter, and Red landed awkwardly in the middle of it with his head down—launching Dani out of the saddle and into the wooden fence around the ring.

"Oh, no!" someone yelled.

Tommi was already jumping out of her saddle. She was the closest to Dani, who'd landed hard and was lying still.

"Stay here," she ordered Legs, not really caring whether he obeyed.

She sprinted to the fallen rider's side. Dani was groaning, her eyes blinking rapidly as she stared at the clear summer sky.

"Keep still," Tommi ordered, channeling Jamie. "Don't try to move yet."

A second later Jamie himself skidded to his knees on Dani's other side. "Can you hear me?" he asked, touching her shoulder. "Did you hit your head?"

"Um, I don't think so." Dani winced, trying to prop herself up on her elbows. "Ow."

Tommi glanced back just long enough to see that Kate had already jumped off and caught Red, who was prancing and rolling his eyes but seemed to be okay. Fitz had hopped off, too, holding Legs along with his own horse.

"Is she okay?" Summer called out.

Jamie didn't answer. Hearing a groan, Tommi turned back to see the trainer running his hands down one of Dani's legs. There was a big scrape on her left boot, and both knees of her breeches were trashed.

"Ow!" Dani yelped when Jamie gently squeezed her left calf.

Jamie's expression was grim. "Keep her still, Tommi," he ordered, pulling out his phone. "I'm calling an ambulance. I think that leg is broken."

THREE

— — — — —

"Mmm, that was delicious." Zara's mother dabbed at her lips with a snowy white linen napkin. "I'm glad you suggested this, love. Even if the restaurant wasn't your first choice." She winked playfully at Zara.

Zara forced a smile. Okay, so at least Gina seemed to believe the whole La Vache Folle had been a joke. Ha freaking ha. The joke had been on Zara when she'd arrived a few minutes early, only to find that what she'd assumed was some chic little French bistro was actually a retro-lame dive bar, complete with peanut shells on the floor. Okay, so according to Zagat's the food was "delish." Still, not exactly her mother's scene.

Luckily there was a fancy Italian place right across the street, and the maître d' had taken one look at Gina and led them to the best table in the house. Unfortunately for Zara, the celebrity service continued, with an attentive waiter appearing almost instantly to take their order and their food appearing at record speed. Sneaking a peek at her watch, Zara saw that it had barely been an hour and a half since she'd left the loft. Not long enough.

"Um, I'm still hungry," she blurted out. Glancing around for their waiter, she waved at him. "I knew I should've ordered another side—the lobster ravioli was way too small. Can I get something else?" She glanced around at nearby tables for inspiration. "Uh, the calamari looks good."

Gina looked surprised, but she shrugged and settled back in her chair. "Whatever you like, my darling girl. I'm just so happy to see your gorgeous face again! I've missed you."

"Yeah, me too." Zara smiled distractedly as her mother reached across the table and squeezed her hand, mentally calculating how much longer until it was safe to go home.

A little over an hour later, Zara held her breath as the cab turned the corner and the loft came into sight. Leaning forward, she scanned both sides of the street. No sign of the bright yellow truck with the cleaning company logo on it. Thank God. She'd stalled as long as she could, eating the calamari one bite at a time, then talking Gina into splitting a couple of desserts. By the time the check finally came, she was so full she never wanted to see tiramisu again.

But it had been worth it. Mission accomplished.

"I can't wait to see the place again!" Gina peered out over Zara's shoulder. "That's the building, right?"

"Yeah, that's it." Zara had almost forgotten that her mother had only seen the loft once. She'd been on location since before Zara and Zac had officially moved in. Good. That meant she wouldn't miss the broken vase or the rug that had had to be sent out for deep cleaning or the antique table clock that had mysteriously disappeared during one of Stacie's weekend-long parties.

Soon they were stepping into the loft. It smelled a whole lot better than when Zara had left. Good. Somehow, Eau de Puke didn't seem like the best way to welcome her mother to New York.

Gina slung her leather weekend bag onto the floor under the foyer's built-in counter, then stepped out into the main room, her Balenciaga heels clicking on the polished hardwood. "The light is wonderful in here!" she exclaimed. "And I love what you and your father have done with the place!"

"Yeah, Zac made sure to hire some hotshot decorator to do it up right." Zara glanced around. The cleaners had done a good job. The place was spotless, but a copy of *New York* magazine was lying open on the coffee table and Zara's scuffed flannel slippers were peeking out from under the sofa. She flopped onto the nearest chair, relieved. She'd done it. She'd had to eat half of New York City along the way, but she'd done it.

Gina stepped over and gave her a light squeeze on the shoulder. "Aren't you going to give me the grand tour, love?"

"Oh." Zara stood up. "Um, okay, sure. This is obviously the living room or whatever." She waved a hand to encompass the huge main room with its floor-to-ceiling windows. "Lots of space for all Zac's minions to hang out and watch TV and pick their toenails and stuff."

Gina chuckled. "Yes, that sounds about right. Is that the kitchen over there?"

"Uh-huh." Zara trailed along as her mother hurried into the galley kitchen.

"I remember this." Gina touched the countertop. "I thought it looked a bit industrial, all this concrete and stainless steel. But your father adored it. Said it was easy to clean."

Zara rolled her eyes. She was pretty sure the last time either of her parents had cleaned anything was sometime in the previous millennium. If then.

"Want to see upstairs?" she asked, already heading back out of the kitchen, which smelled strongly of bleach and lemon-scented cleaning crap. She didn't want Gina to notice and start asking questions about that, since Zara wasn't exactly known as a fan of random cleaning herself.

She led the way up the airy wood-and-steel staircase. At the top was a long, narrow gangway of a hall, one side overlooking the main room and the other lined with doorways.

"Here's my room." Zara flung open one of the doors.

"Very nice." Gina stepped in and looked around. "And very neat! Who are you, and what have you done with my daughter? Because *my* darling Zara has never made her bed a day in her life!" She let out her famous musical laugh, the one that had charmed every leading man in Hollywood. Or so her publicist said, anyway.

Zara rolled her eyes. "No biggie," she muttered, feeling uncomfortable. "Uh, Stacie's a real neat freak. It's easier to, like, make the bed or whatever than to listen to her bitching."

Gina smiled. "Nice to hear she's such a good influence. Where is she, anyway? I was hoping she'd be here to welcome us—I'm dying to meet her."

"Oh!" Zara was ready for this, but she still felt herself go all tense. "Guess I forgot to tell you earlier. She's, uh, not here right now."

"Not here?" One of Gina's sculpted eyebrows went up. "What do you mean?"

"She's off at some two-day interview for some kind of internship thing." Zara had practiced her story in her head during the cab ride uptown, but was still a little surprised by how easily it rolled off her tongue. Score one for genetics— obviously she'd inherited some of her mother's acting skills. "They're putting her up in some hotel out in New Jersey or somewhere and making her meet with a bunch of people. Anyway, she was totally psyched about it."

Gina looked dubious. "I see," she said. "So she left you all alone here in the city?"

"Yeah, but only because she knew you were coming home," Zara said quickly. "See, they called her about this interview last week, only she didn't get to talk to them because we were out at a movie, and . . ." She swallowed hard, realizing she was rambling. Duh. The first rule of a good lie? Keep it short and simple. Not too many details. "Anyway, it doesn't matter. The point is, we found out you were coming home just in time. She still wasn't sure—she's, like, totally Miss Responsibility, it's super lame. But I told her I could survive the, like, three hours I'd be on my own in the big bad city until you got here. Practically had to shove her out the door this morning."

"I see," Gina said again. This time she sounded a little confused. Zara decided that was an improvement.

"Come on—your room's next," she said, hurrying down the hall.

They checked out the master bedroom suite, then moved on to the guest room beyond. "So is this where Cousin Stacie is staying?" Gina asked as she peered into the latter. "You're right, she *is* very tidy, isn't she?"

"Yeah, like I said." Zara gulped as she glanced around the room, which showed no signs it had ever been occupied. What if Gina wandered into the bathroom and noticed that there wasn't so much as a toothbrush or a bottle of shampoo in there?

She shot her mother a nervous glance, but Gina was already turning away. "Did I see an answering machine downstairs?" she asked. "I gave my agent's assistant this number in case they couldn't reach me on the plane."

"Yeah. It's in that little nook thingy by the front door. Zac calls it the message center." Zara followed her mother back downstairs, still feeling anxious.

Was this whole stupid cover-up really worth it? Maybe she should just come clean, tell Gina what had really happened with Stacie.

She perched on the edge of the couch while Gina hurried out to the message center. Ignoring the sound of the machine clicking on, Zara flipped through the issue of *New York* magazine and tried to figure out what to do.

She snapped out of it when she heard a familiar voice coming out of the machine's tinny little speakers. "Hello, this is Joy from Pelham Lane Stables calling for Zara," the assistant trainer's chirpy-happy voice said. "We're just checking in to remind you that you were scheduled to ride in the group lesson today, and we were surprised not to see you. Please call to let us know you're all right."

Oops. Zara reached for her cell phone, belatedly

remembering that she'd switched it off after receiving two more texts from Grant in the cab on her way to meet her mother. She turned it back on. Four voice mails, nine texts. Three of the texts and one of the voice messages were from Grant. But there were also two messages from Joy and one text from Tommi.

Gina stepped back into the main room and frowned at her. "What was that all about?"

"Guess I forgot." Zara stuck her phone in her pocket. "No biggie. The new barn's just really uptight about that stuff."

"It's not *uptight* for them to expect you to turn up for a scheduled lesson." Gina crossed her arms over her chest, suddenly looking more like a sour-faced mom than a movie star. "We pay a lot of money to that barn every month, Zara. The least you could do is try to be a little more responsible about meeting your obligations."

Zara rolled her eyes. "Like I said, I just forgot, okay? So sue me for being distracted 'cause you're coming home for the first time in a million years. Anyway, it's the first lesson I've missed all summer, so I don't know why everyone's freaking out about it."

Gina sighed. "I hope that's true. And if it is, I expect we can thank your cousin Stacie for keeping you on track this long. It just goes to show how important it is that you have a good role model around while your father and I are away."

"Whatever," Zara muttered.

That answered that question. There was no way she could tell her mother the truth about Stacie. No. Way.

Because if Gina knew that Stacie wasn't exactly the role model she thought she was, she'd never let Zara stay in New

York on her own. She'd probably whisk her off to Vancouver with her when she returned.

Or, actually, *not*. With school due to start up in a few short weeks, she was more likely to hire a *real* nanny to come stay until her movie wrapped or Zac's tour finished, whichever came first. And while Gina had originally become famous by playing the pretty, sassy-ditzy sidekick in a series of successful romantic comedies, Zara knew that her mother wasn't nearly as airheaded as she came across. She wouldn't slack off on checking references the way Zac had.

"I'm sorry, okay?" she blurted out. "You're totally right. I've been relying on Stacie to keep me on track, and I guess I just spaced after she left today. My bad."

Gina sighed. "All right, thank you for apologizing, love. I just hope some of your cousin's responsibility rubs off on you this summer. You're almost seventeen now, and you'll be heading out on your own to college in just a couple of short years . . ."

Zara could see tears welling up in her mother's big, gold-flecked brown eyes. That was another thing that had helped Gina Girard become a star. Being able to cry on cue. And look pretty doing it.

"Right," Zara said quickly, hoping to head off the water-works. "I mean, Stacie and I have been spending tons of time together, so I'm sure she's been a great influence."

Okay, so the first part was true. She and Stacie *had* spent plenty of time together. The good influence part? Did Stacie teaching Zara how to make a bunch of drinks she'd never tried before count?

She couldn't help feeling a twinge of guilt as her mother

wandered back out to the message center. Yeah, she was still mad at Stacie for ditching her, but she was also starting to worry about the girl a little. Should she have called the cops or something when she disappeared? Or at least Googled the guy she ran off with to make sure he wasn't a serial killer or something? Not that she could do that, since she didn't even know his last name . . .

She shrugged that off, trying not to worry about it. She could try texting or e-mailing her cousin later to make sure she was alive. In the meantime she had to convince Gina that Stacie was still around.

So just exactly how was she supposed to pull *that* off for an entire week?

"Any pepperoni left?" Fitz leaned over the pizza boxes on the big bandage trunk in the middle of the tack room.

Tommi glanced up from her position on a stool nearby. The traditional post-lesson pizza fest was pretty subdued today. No wonder. After the ambulance had arrived to take Dani away, Jamie had tried to continue. But everyone was so distracted that it didn't seem safe to jump. They'd just done some more flatwork for a while before finally giving up and calling it a day.

"There was only one more slice," Tommi told Fitz. "But Goldie put her feet up on the box and drooled on it, so I gave it to her."

She gestured at the yellow-and-white collie mix sitting alertly at her feet. As usual, several of the barn's resident dogs were circling the pizza hopefully. Summer's obnoxious Jack Russell, Whiskey, was among them, though he seemed more interested in snapping at the other dogs than in scrounging for pizza.

"Should someone go see if Jamie's okay?" Marissa spoke up, picking a piece of mushroom off her slice. "He seemed pretty shaken up after they took Dani away."

"No wonder," Kate put in quietly. "It's been a long time since there's been a serious injury at Pelham Lane."

Marissa shuddered. "I can still hear Dani's poor leg cracking when she hit that fence."

"You can not." Fitz rolled his eyes. "Don't be such a drama queen."

"I'm not! I really did hear it!" Marissa insisted. "I just didn't want to say anything until we knew if it was really broken."

"Well, we know now," Summer pointed out.

Tommi nodded. Jamie had called the hospital for an update while they were waiting for the pizza to arrive. Dani's leg was indeed fractured, and the doctors were still trying to decide whether she needed surgery.

"I wonder if they had to cut her boots off," Marissa said. "I hope not. They're practically new—she got them for her birthday in May."

Just then Tommi's phone buzzed. She pulled it out of the pocket of her Tailored Sportsmans and saw that it was a text from Brooke.

Update: Abby's driving. We leave at 9 on Friday. You in?

Tommi stuck the phone back in her pocket without answering. She still hadn't decided what to do about that weekend.

She reached over to grab a napkin off the bandage trunk. As she did, she saw that Kate was only picking at the slice of pizza in her lap. She'd pulled off all the cheese, leaving it in a sticky, greasy blob at the edge of the paper plate. Now she was pulling off chunks of the crust.

Tommi picked up a slice of plain cheese and stepped around the trunk. Fitz and Marissa were arguing about how much pain they'd be willing to endure to save their own boots, and Summer was fiddling with Whiskey's collar, so none of them paid any attention to what she was doing.

"Hey," Tommi said softly, sliding the new slice onto Kate's plate. "Thought you might want this."

Kate frowned and glanced up sharply. Then she relaxed and nodded.

"Thanks," she said. Lifting the new slice, she took a small bite, then another.

Tommi smiled and moved back to her seat, figuring that was good enough. None of them felt much like eating right now.

"I have an idea," Fitz said, clapping his hands. "In honor of Dani's fall, let's all describe our most humiliating and painful riding accidents. I'll start—though it might be hard to narrow down the options. Shall I begin with the time I fell off because I forgot to tighten my girth? See, I was kind of sleepy that day, and—"

"I have a better idea," Summer interrupted. "I know something that will definitely cheer you all up."

"What's that?" Marissa asked.

"My big announcement." Summer preened as all eyes turned to her. "Obviously I didn't get to make it during our lesson like I planned, so I might as well do it now."

Tommi rolled her eyes. Summer had been hinting all day that she had some big secret to share. She could only imagine what it was—probably something about getting a new saddle or the custom chaps she'd been grousing that her parents wouldn't buy her.

Summer didn't leave them in suspense for long. "So here it is: I'm having a huge Sweet Sixteen party, and you're all invited!"

"A party? I'm in." Fitz grinned, though even he seemed to be having trouble mustering up much enthusiasm for Summer's news.

Summer didn't appear to notice the underwhelming response. "My birthday just happens to be a week from Friday—in other words, right during the Washington Crossing show," she went on. "So my parents are renting out the mansion on the showgrounds—well, like half of it, anyway." She giggled. "And also part of the gardens and stuff, too. There's going to be an awesome live band, and some famous surprise guests, and tons of amazing food . . ."

There was more, but Tommi tuned it out. She had too much stuff to think about already, like making sure Kate kept eating, hoping Dani was okay, figuring out which classes she and Legs should do at the big show, and deciding what to do about Brooke's invitation.

Some goofy over-the-top Summer party? Not even on her radar.

FOUR

— — — — —

"What do you think? Is it me?" Court held up a slinky scoop-neck T and glanced toward the mirrored back wall of the Upper East Side boutique.

Tommi tilted her head. "I don't know. The color's okay, but the sleeves—hold on." Hearing a buzz, she fished in her Kooba hobo bag for her phone.

"Oh, God." Court rolled her eyes. "Another text from Mr. Wonderful?"

Tommi grinned and shrugged. "What can I say? He likes to keep in touch."

She checked her phone. Sure enough, it was a text from Alex.

what do u want me to play for u during my set tomorrow night? I'll dedicate it to the coolest girl in nyc.

Court slung the T-shirt back on the shelf and stepped over to peek at the text. "Ugh," she said. "You two are so cute it's disgusting."

"I know, right?" Tommi quickly tapped out her response: *you decide on the right song for me—ur the pro, right?*

She tucked the phone in her purse. "Okay, where were we?" she said, glancing around the store.

She and Court were the only customers in the place at the moment. Not that it was getting them much attention from the young, bored-looking salesclerk. She was perched on a stool behind the funky mosaic-studded counter, totally ignoring them as she flipped through a magazine.

"We were talking about why you're even thinking about not coming to Penn with us this weekend." Court wandered toward a rack of dresses.

Tommi sighed. "I told you, I'm thinking about it," she said. "It's just that I've got a lot going on right now with this horse—"

"Horse, schmorse." Court grabbed a spaghetti-strap mini, held it up against herself, and eyed the result in the mirrored wall. "How many times does one of your best friends leave for college?"

She had a point. They'd all been friends for ages, even though Brooke was a year ahead of Tommi and Court in school. It was hard to believe she was about to leave for college in a whole different city.

"Anyway, it's going to be a blast." Court started flipping through the dresses. "Brooke can't move into the dorm for like another week or two, so she's staying with her cousin until then. He's going to be a junior at Penn this year, and he lives in this house off-campus with a bunch of other guys." She shot a look at Tommi. "You haven't met Cousin Jon before, have you?"

Tommi shrugged. "I don't think so."

"That's a no for sure," Court said. "Trust me, if you'd met him, you'd remember. He's überhot. I already told Parker that if Juicy Jon even looks at me this weekend, we're through."

Tommi grinned. Court and their other longtime friend Parker had become a couple earlier that summer. Their relationship consisted mostly of making fun of each other and threatening to break up for various goofy reasons. Tommi didn't quite get it, but it seemed to work for the two of them.

"Poor Parker," she teased. "I'm sure he's really worried."

"Whatever. You haven't seen Cousin Jon." Court smirked. "Anyway, it's just one more reason you should come."

"Okay. But it doesn't change the fact that I have stuff I need to be doing right here in New York. I can't just run off for the weekend on a whim." Even as she said it, Tommi couldn't help thinking about a certain recent trip to the Hamptons. Alex had invited her out for a house party at his place, and she hadn't been able to resist, even though it meant missing the beginning of the last show and skipping a schooling jumpers class she'd intended to do with Legs.

"Well, you'd better make up your mind. In case you forgot, we're leaving in less than forty-eight hours." Court pulled out another dress. "How's this one on me? Think the college boys will like it?"

Before Tommi could answer, her phone buzzed again.

ok, I'll pick a song for u, Alex wrote. *If u like it, maybe it can be our song.*

"Wait," Court said, turning away from the dresses. "How stupid am I? This doesn't have anything to do with that horse, does it? You just don't want to spend a whole weekend away from your sexy new boy toy!"

Tommi rolled her eyes. "So not it."

"No, I'm totally right!" Court grinned, grabbing a nearby mannequin and pretending to smooch on it. "Tommi doesn't want to go on some lame girls-only trip and leave her *lov-ah* behind!"

"Shut up." Tommi gave her a playful shove. "That's got nothing to do with it. Now are you going to try on any of this stuff or not?"

An hour later, Tommi slung her shopping bags over one wrist and dug in her bag for her keys with the other hand. "Hurry up," Court urged, bouncing from foot to foot on the town house's front steps. "I can't hold it much longer!"

"I'm trying." Tommi's hand finally closed on her keys. She opened the door, then stepped aside to let Court push past her and dash for the powder room under the stairs.

"Thank God!" Court exclaimed as she slammed the bathroom door behind her.

Tommi grinned, then stepped into the hall to set her bags on the antique French console table. It had been a productive morning of shopping—she'd found a lot of fun new school clothes, bought a get-well gift for Dani, and even picked up a dress to wear to Summer's big party. She and Court had ended up with so many bags that they'd decided to swing by Tommi's place to drop them off before heading to lunch.

Checking her watch, Tommi saw that they should have just enough time for a leisurely meal at her favorite neighborhood bistro before she had to leave for the barn. She was glad. It had been nice to reconnect with Court one-on-one—so far this summer, she'd mostly seen her at parties or other big group things. Of course, if she went on that trip to Penn she'd get to spend the whole weekend reconnecting with Brooke and the others, too . . .

Hearing the shuffle of feet at the end of the hall, she glanced up, expecting to see Mrs. Grigoryan. Instead, her father appeared in the doorway. He was dressed in a business suit and a pair of leather slippers, with his reading glasses perched on the end of his nose and a sheaf of papers in one hand.

"Dad," Tommi said. "What are you doing here?"

Her father took a step forward. "What do you mean, what am I doing here? It's my house, isn't it?" He grinned and winked.

Tommi rolled her eyes. So her dad was in one of his goofy, playful moods. That probably meant he'd just closed some huge business deal or taken over another company or something.

Just then Court burst out of the powder room, still fastening her beaded belt. "Whew! My bladder's feeling much better now. I—oh! Hi, Mr. A." Court grinned sheepishly as she saw Tommi's father standing there. "What's up?"

"Hello, Courtney." Tommi's father nodded to her. "Haven't seen you around much lately. Keeping yourself busy this summer, are you?"

"Trying." Court shrugged, then stepped over and linked her arm through Tommi's. "Trying to keep Tommi a little busier, too—I just spent all morning trying to talk her into riding down to help Brooke move onto campus this weekend."

"Shut up," Tommi hissed at her.

Too late. She could see her father's eyes light up. "Campus?" he echoed. "What are you talking about? Thomasina? What's she talking about?"

"It's nothing, Dad," Tommi said. "Brooke's getting ready to start college down at Penn, and Court and a couple of other people are going along to help her move in."

"And Tommi's invited, too," Court put in. "Only we can't convince her to take one measly weekend off from her horses. Maybe you can talk some sense into her, Mr. A?"

"I see." Mr. Aaronson was still gazing intently at Tommi. "Tommi didn't mention it to me."

Tommi gritted her teeth, already planning out the various forms of horrible torture she had in store for Court later. There was a reason she hadn't told her father about the trip—she knew he'd get all college rah-rah and insist she go. And she had a feeling he was about to demonstrate that.

"It's just that I'm not sure I have time right now," she began. "We leave for the Washington Crossing show next week, and Legs—"

"Nonsense," her father cut her off. "It's only two days, and—"

"Three, actually," Court broke in. "We're leaving Friday morning and coming back sometime on Monday."

Normally Tommi's father hated being interrupted. But he just smiled and nodded. "Even better," he said. "It'll be good for you to take a break from the horses for a weekend, Thomasina. See what other options are out there if this little experiment of yours doesn't work out. Or even if it does, for that matter."

"But Legs—"

"Is a horse," her father said. "And one that pricey trainer of yours is perfectly capable of riding for you if he needs it." He reached out and gave her shoulder a squeeze. "I'll let

Mrs. Grigoryan know you won't be here for dinners this weekend. In fact, it may be a good time to give her a weekend off—your stepmother and I can eat out for a few days." He smiled. "Nice seeing you again, Courtney."

"You too, Mr. A," Court said. Tommi shot her a glare, but Court just grinned back at her. "Great, so you're going," she sing-songed as Tommi's father hurried away. "Better start packing."

"What's wrong with his feet?" Summer asked.

Kate set down the horse's hoof and gave him a pat before answering. "He's got a little thrush," she said with as much patience as she could. She straightened up and stretched before capping the bottle of Thrush Buster. Her shoulders were sore thanks to the pair of rowdy ponies she'd just brought in from turnout.

"Oh. What's thrush?"

Kate gritted her teeth, mentally counting to ten before answering this time. How had Summer managed to own horses for years without learning the most basic things about them? Then again, paying attention to that sort of stuff would eat up valuable gossiping and bragging time . . .

Normally Kate found Summer pretty easy to ignore, but today it was a challenge. Summer had been following Kate around for the past fifteen minutes, prattling on about her stupid Sweet Sixteen party. Kate was pretty sure it was only because none of the other juniors were around, but that didn't make it any easier to take. She had a ton to do as usual, even though she'd arrived extra early that morning.

Which was part of the problem, actually. Kate was always eager to get to the barn. But that morning she'd been even more eager to get away from her house, which was still pretty much a war zone. That was why she'd set her alarm for 5:00 a.m. and sneaked out before her parents were awake. Her brother? She had no idea if he was awake or even at home. All she knew was that there'd been no sound from his basement bedroom as she tiptoed around, getting ready to go.

"Well?" Summer sounded impatient.

Kate stifled a yawn, realizing she was drifting. What had Summer asked her again? Something stupid, no doubt . . .

"Never mind, I don't care," Summer went on before Kate could dredge up the answer. "Anyway, did I tell you? I'm thinking of getting Whiskey a little pink tux that matches the dress I'm wearing for my party. Doesn't that sound cute?"

"Hmm," Kate said, feeling on safer ground. As long as Summer was talking about herself, she didn't usually bother to notice whether anyone was paying attention. Unhooking the horse from the cross-ties, she led him toward his stall nearby.

Summer drifted along beside her. "I was actually thinking about asking everyone to wear white to the party—you know, so my dress would really stand out. It's pink, you know. Mom hired Chelly Swain to design it for me."

She paused, seeming to expect a response to that. Kate finished hooking the horse's stall guard, then forced a smile. "Really?" she said.

"You know who she is, right?" Summer said. "I mean, she's only the hottest new fashion designer in New York!" She shrugged. "But anyway, my dad talked me out of the white thing. He said it would be too hard to convince so many people to do it. I mean, there will probably be at least, like, three hundred guests."

"Wow," Kate said, since Summer had paused again.

"Yeah," Summer said, following as Kate headed toward the tack room. "It's going to be huge. Lots of celebrities and VIPs and stuff. But don't worry, even *you* will probably know a bunch of people, since I invited the whole barn."

Kate forced a smile. She wasn't even sure she'd bother to go to the party. Fitz seemed interested—he said it was sure to be a spectacle—but shows were always so busy, and Kate would have tons to do. Why waste time watching Summer show off her parents' money?

As if on cue, Fitz appeared at the end of the aisle. "I've been looking all over for you!" he exclaimed, hurrying over and wrapping his arms around Kate.

"Aw, so sweet!" Summer simpered.

Fitz shot her a grin. "Hey, Summer, not to be rude, but Kate and I need a moment. If you know what I mean." Leaning down, he nibbled gently on Kate's earlobe.

"Of course!" Summer giggled. "See you guys later. Don't do anything I wouldn't do!"

"No promises." Fitz grinned and gave Kate another squeeze.

Summer hurried off, and Fitz dragged Kate into the tack room. "Look," Kate said, pushing away from him. "This isn't the best time. I'm supposed to be lungeing that new import horse right now."

"No, you're not." Fitz stepped over to the wall and grabbed a bridle off one of the hooks. "I asked Miguel to take care of it.

—

Because you've got something much more important to do. And you've made me wait long enough already."

Kate's tired mind immediately flashed to that awkward, confusing night in the hay stall. She should have known he wouldn't wait forever; he wasn't the patient type . . .

Then she shook her head, realizing that didn't make sense. If Fitz was looking to fool around right now, why had he just pulled one of his saddles off its rack?

"Here, carry this for a sec," Fitz said, shoving the bridle at her.

Kate took it, watching as he balanced his Delgrange saddle on one hip while digging through his tack trunk. It was a mess, as usual.

"What are you doing?" she asked.

"Looking for Beacon's old splint boots," he said, his voice muffled due to the fact that his head was halfway in the trunk. "I think they should fit Flame."

"Flame?" Kate echoed, her mind moving like molasses.

Fitz's head popped out, displaying a big grin. "Found 'em," he said, holding up a pair of dusty horse boots. "And yeah, Flame. He's had enough time to settle in. Today we're going to see what he can do!"

Kate opened her mouth to protest, then shut it again. She could tell by the look in Fitz's eye that it was no use. Besides, she had to admit that Flame really did seem pretty well settled in already. Almost as if he'd always been there. Why wait?

"Okay," she said. "Let's go see what he can do."

There was nobody in the smaller of the two outdoor rings except a barn cat sunning itself on the mounting block. Kate stopped Flame just outside the gate as Fitz stepped forward to undo the latch. The chestnut stood with his head up and his ears swiveling back and forth as he took in the sights. Kate jiggled the reins lightly to remind him that she was there.

"What do you think, boy?" she murmured. "It's just a ring— just like the one at your old barn."

"Only bigger, right? Maybe he thinks it's a really small race-track," Fitz joked as he swung the gate open. "He's probably looking for the starting gate."

Flame followed Kate into the ring without hesitation, still looking around with obvious interest. When he spotted the cat he surged forward, stretching his neck as he nosed curiously at it. The cat drew back with a look of disgust, then jumped down and ran off.

"Aw, Flame's just trying to make friends!" Fitz called after it with a laugh. Then he turned to Kate. "Ready to hop up there?"

"Yeah, I guess." Kate clicked the snap on her helmet, then slid a hand under Flame's girth to make sure it was snug.

Fitz gave her a leg up, then stepped back. "You okay? I'll be over there." He waved a hand in the direction of the gate.

Kate barely noticed him walking away. All her focus was on the horse beneath her. She'd ridden hundreds of different horses in her riding career so far, but this moment never got old. Those very first few minutes on a new one, the first chance to figure out how to communicate with another individual with a whole new set of quirks and preferences and training. She loved that moment. *Loved* it.

"Walk on," she murmured, with a tiny pulse of her calves on the horse's sides.

Flame's ears flicked back to her, and he stepped off into a forward, ground-covering walk. Kate kept her hands soft, mostly using shifts of her weight to steer him over to the rail.

"Gooooood," she crooned, pleased with how he was responding so far. She let her body follow the motion of his walk, making one loop of the ring and then turning around to do it in the other direction.

"Let's see him trot!" Fitz called out after a few minutes.

She shot him a look and nodded. She was eager to try the faster gait herself. "Trrrrrot," she said, asking Flame to move out with a whisper of pressure from both legs.

This time Flame hesitated, once again flicking his ears toward her as if confirming what she was asking. When she squeezed again, a little harder this time, he surged forward into the trot. At first his head was high and his gait was rushed and tense, as if he was expecting her to grab his mouth at any moment. Kate couldn't blame him. At that show where Kate had first seen the horse, Nat had spent most of her time in the ring hauling back on both reins to keep Flame from running over the short-strided ponies in there with him.

"E-e-e-easy, baby," she whispered. "It's okay. Easy."

She kept her hands light, not taking up any contact on the bit at all at first, doing only as much as she had to do to keep him on the rail. By the time they made it halfway around the ring, Flame was already starting to relax. His ears flicked back and forth as his gait slowed, lengthened, and gained cadence. His head dropped, his neck stretching forward and his nose poking out as his hooves skimmed gracefully over the footing.

Kate smiled, posting effortlessly with the horse's long, flowing stride. Flame's trot felt just as good as it looked. And that was saying something.

After they'd gone around the ring once each direction to warm up, she started working him a little harder, doing some circles and figure eights and a few baby lateral movements. He didn't always understand what she was asking for on the first try, but he obviously wanted to figure it out. By the time Kate asked him to canter, the two of them were working together as if this were their hundredth ride instead of their first.

"Good boy!" Kate cried as she brought the horse down from the right lead canter. The depart had been a little rougher than the one to the left, the canter a little speedy, but that was to be expected with a former racehorse. And once he was in it, the gait had been just as fluid as the rest.

She was leaning forward to give Flame a pat when she noticed that Tommi had joined Fitz at the rail. Riding toward them, Kate let the reins slide to the buckle so Flame could stretch his head down and relax.

"Is this your first time on him?" Tommi asked when Kate and Flame got closer.

"Yeah," Fitz answered before Kate could open her mouth. "Isn't she doing great? I swear, Kate could ride the hair off a rhinoceros!"

Tommi nodded, never taking her eyes off Flame. "That horse is no rhinoceros," she said. "I mean, you can tell he doesn't know much. But check out the way he moves!"

"I know." Kate gave Flame another pat as he snuffled at

Tommi over the fence, clearly looking for treats. "It's obvious from the first step, isn't it?"

"To you geniuses, maybe." Fitz grinned. "Good thing I had the most beautiful and talented rider in the tristate area with me to help me see it that first time."

Tommi snorted. "Laying it on a little thick, aren't you?" she asked Fitz. "Kate already seems to tolerate you, so you probably don't need the flattery."

Kate could feel Flame getting restless, so she nudged him back into a walk and then a trot, leaving Fitz and Tommi bickering happily at the rail. She didn't want to overdo it on their very first ride, but she figured it wouldn't hurt to do a little more trot work and then call it a day.

When she pulled up again a few minutes later, she was grinning from ear to ear. "You are such a good boy," she whispered to the horse, rubbing his neck with both hands as she leaned forward to swing her leg over and dismount. She was on the ground running up her stirrups when she saw that Jamie had now joined Tommi and Fitz. The trainer was leaning on the arena fence, his astute blue eyes focused on Flame.

"What do you think?" Kate asked him as she led the horse over.

"He's got potential, definitely." Jamie reached over to rub the horse's face. "Like I told Fitz, you've got a good eye, Kate. If this guy jumps half as nicely as he moves, he'll make a hunter for sure."

Fitz nodded. "Maybe next time we can pop him over a crossrail or two. You know—just to see what we've got."

"Maybe." Kate shot a look at Jamie as he swung open the

gate. Did he really think Flame had what it took to be a top hunter?

Even the thought of it made it a little easier to forget that she still hadn't heard from Natalie. Easier to ignore the flash of guilt every time she remembered how proud Nat had been of her new project at the show that day.

Because despite all of it, Kate couldn't help being glad— *really* glad—that Flame was here.

FIVE

—— —— —— —— ——

Zara's nerves jangled as she climbed out of the car. "Thanks, dude," she said to the driver, a swarthy little guy who'd hummed tunelessly the entire way from SoHo to Pelham Lane, though the radio wasn't even on. Annoying, but Zara had been too distracted to notice much. "Just hang out here and wait for me, okay?" she told him. "I'll be a couple of hours, probably."

"You got it, miss." The driver pulled out a copy of the *Post* and leaned back in his seat, already starting up with the humming again.

Zara closed the door behind her, not bothering to calculate how much it was going to cost to keep the hired car there while she rode. A lot more than having Stacie drop her off and then pick her up, but whatever. That fell under the umbrella of Not Her Problem.

She was heading toward the barn when she noticed a cluster of people up by one of the outdoor rings. One of those people was Jamie.

"Here goes nothing, I guess," Zara muttered under her breath, changing directions.

She'd spent most of the drive up here trying to plan out what she was going to say to her trainer. Jamie was a tough one to read. He could be a real hardass sometimes. Most of the time, actually.

Then again, he kept giving Zara chances when even she wasn't sure she deserved them. Like the time she'd been caught smoking in one of the outbuildings. The various times she'd been late or mouthed off in lessons. The time he'd found her getting busy in a stall with one of the part-time muckers.

And of course there was the thing with that horse Ford. But that was different. Jamie didn't know she'd had anything to do with that. He seemed to actually believe Fitz's story. Go figure.

She pushed that aside as Jamie turned and saw her coming. "Zara," he said.

"Hi," Zara blurted out. "Listen, Jamie, I'm really sorry about missing yesterday's lesson. See, my mom decided to fly home from Vancouver for a surprise visit, and I guess I just totally spaced. I'm really, really sorry—I swear it won't happen again."

Jamie had a little frown on his face as he listened, but then he nodded. "Fine," he said, running a hand over his hair, even though every strand was gelled perfectly into place as usual. "See that it doesn't. But apology accepted—this time."

"Cool." Zara let out a sigh of relief as Jamie checked his watch.

"Got to go," the trainer said. "Got a lesson in the indoor in five." He reached over to pat the tall, gangly chestnut Fitz was leading. "Glad I got to see this guy go."

Tommi watched Jamie hurry off, then turned to Zara. "You got off easy," she said. "He was pretty pissed when you didn't show yesterday."

"Yeah." Zara shrugged. "So what'd I miss?"

"Kind of a lot, actually," Fitz said. "Dani's horse pitched her into the fence and broke her leg."

Zara rolled her eyes. "Yeah, right."

"No, Fitz is telling the truth for once," Tommi said. "See, they were doing this tricky four stride line, and . . ." She went on to describe the accident, with Fitz jumping in to add a few gory details. Kate didn't have much to say, as usual, though she nodded along with the story.

"Whoa," Zara said when they finished. "That's a serious bummer." She didn't know Dani all that well, but the girl seemed pretty hyper. Being stuck in a cast for however many weeks couldn't be fun for someone like that. Or anyone, really.

She drifted along as the others led the horse down the tidy stone dust path toward the barn.

"So where were you yesterday, anyway?" Fitz asked. "Is that true about your mom?"

"Every word, believe it or not." Zara grimaced. "Although I may have left a few things out. Like my idiot cousin, for instance . . ."

She quickly told them the rest. How Stacie had fooled Zac into thinking she was some paragon of responsibility. How as soon as he was out of sight, she'd traded in her khakis for skankwear and started hitting the clubs and throwing parties at the loft every night. How she'd taken off with some random guy over the weekend, leaving Zara to cover for her.

"So do you really think you can pull it off?" Tommi asked when she'd finished. "Hide the whole Stacie thing from your mom?"

"We'll find out, I guess." Zara was tired of talking about it. It was bad enough she had to live it. "Anyway, I figured I'd better come see my horses just in case I end up grounded for life or something."

Fitz grinned and gave a light tug on the lead line as the tall, skinny chestnut stretched his long neck toward the grass growing beside the path. "Come on, Kate, let's get our big boy inside and cleaned up."

"Yeah." Kate smiled and rubbed the horse's face as it turned and nuzzled at her. She looked even spacier than usual, and Zara wondered if she'd heard anything the rest of them had said in the past five minutes.

The barn's big double doors were standing open to catch any stray breeze that might cut the stifling August heat. Zara hung back to let the horse and his little band of groupies enter the barn first, then peeled off in the direction of Keeper's stall.

"Later," she called to the others, not bothering to wait for a response. Even though she was starting to think of them as friends, at least sort of, she didn't like to count on them feeling the same. Too easy to get knocked on your ass that way, and she had enough problems right now as it was.

As she rounded the corner, Zara checked her watch. Two thirty already. She'd have to hurry if she wanted to squeeze in a ride today. Or maybe she should just feed Keeper a few carrots and call it a day. She definitely wanted to be there when her mother got home that evening. Not that she had any clue what she was going to tell her this time . . .

"Zara! Oh good, you're here!"

Zara winced. Glancing over her shoulder, she saw Summer rushing toward her with a big, goofy grin on her face.

Summer skidded to a stop beside her. "Where were you yesterday?" she exclaimed. "You totally missed my big news! I'm having a Sweet Sixteen party at the Washington Crossing show! We're renting out the old mansion, and there's going to be a band and like a million guests and really awesome food and—"

"Yeah, I heard," Zara cut her off, putting as much excitement as she felt into her voice. Exactly none.

As usual, Summer didn't seem to notice. "Oh, you heard about it already? That's cool." She beamed. "I guess word spreads fast around here. Especially huge news like this, right? Anyway, you probably heard that, like, the whole barn is invited. But I wanted to make sure to invite you personally, you know? Oh! And there are going to be lots of adults there and stuff, so like, if your parents wanted to come they're totally welcome, too."

Yeah. Of course they were. Zara could only imagine how over-the-top, wet-her-pants psyched Summer would be if Zac Trask and Gina Girard showed up at her dorky little birthday bash.

"Better not alert the paparazzi on that one," Zara told Summer. "They've both made plans to be in other countries to avoid your party."

"What?" Summer's smile faltered. Zara could almost see

the little wheels in the girl's head turning as she tried to figure out whether Zara was joking.

Even though Summer was getting on her nerves as usual, Zara felt a flash of guilt. A tiny one, anyway.

"Kidding. Duh," she said, rolling her eyes. "But yeah, they'll both be out of town then."

"Oh." Summer giggled. "Good one, Zara! You're coming, though, right? I mean, you'll be at the show already, so obviously you'll come. Right?"

Before Zara had to answer, there was a sudden shout from the other end of the barn. It sounded like Fitz.

"What's going on?" Zara wondered. "Hope the new racehorse didn't decide the wash stall looked like a starting gate."

"I know, right?" Summer wrinkled her nose. "What was Fitz thinking, bringing some scrawny half-trained thing like that into the barn?"

Not really the point, but Zara didn't bother explaining. "Let's go see what's up."

She headed down the aisle, not bothering to see if Summer was following. The wash stalls were located in the center block of the barn at the opposite end from the feed room. They consisted of several large, airy bays with drains in the floor and hoses on overhead booms.

At the moment only one of the stalls was occupied. Fitz's new Thoroughbred was watching with pricked ears as Fitz, Kate, and Tommi surrounded someone in the aisle just outside the stall. Zara's eyes widened when she saw who it was.

"Is that Dani?" she said in surprise. "Whoa, didn't think we'd see her around here so soon."

"No kidding," Summer said. Then she rushed forward, shoving Kate aside to grab Dani. "Oh wow, Dani! Welcome back!"

Dani grinned sheepishly, leaning on one crutch to awkwardly return Summer's hug. "Hi, Summer. I figured I'd better stop in and show you all I'm still alive," she joked. "I also want to visit Red and let him know it wasn't his fault and I still love him." When she noticed Zara behind Summer, she lifted one hand. "Hey, Zara," she added. "You totally missed my involuntary dismount yesterday."

"Yeah, I heard it was pretty spectacular." Zara stared at Dani's cast, which covered her left leg from just above her toes to just below the knee. "You okay?"

"She got a nine on the somersault from the Russian judge, but then completely blew the landing," Fitz said.

"Very funny." Dani stuck out her tongue at him.

"Don't listen to him. We're all glad to see you," Kate said softly. Shooting Dani a smile, she ducked under the cross-ties and started working on the horse's far side with a sweat scraper.

"So Marissa said you had to have surgery," Summer said to Dani.

"Yeah, that was fun." Dani grimaced. "But I guess it went okay. I'm not supposed to put any weight on it for a while, but the doctors say I should be okay in about six weeks."

"Six weeks? That's not too bad," Tommi said. "You could be back in the saddle in time for Harrisburg."

"I hope so." Dani leaned on her crutches. "Anyway, I'll probably need all six weeks to convince my parents that I'm not going to—"

"There you are!" a loud voice rang out, cutting her off.

A girl Zara had never seen before stomped toward them. She was about their age, with overprocessed reddish-brown hair and hoochie-mama cutoffs. The girl ignored Zara and the others, her angry gaze focused on the horse in the wash stall. She jabbed a finger at it.

"I can't believe you stole him right out from under me!" she yelled.

Kate took a step out of the stall, gripping her sweat scraper so hard her knuckles were white. "Nat!" she exclaimed.

Kate felt frozen in place. It was like one of those dreams where terrible things happened and she had no idea how to stop them.

Only this time, it was way too real.

"I can't believe it!" Nat exclaimed again, her face bright red as she stared from Flame to Kate and back again. "I mean, even when they told me he was here, I was sure there was some mistake. My so-called *best friend* wouldn't do that to me. No way." Her words dripped with acid.

"Listen, Nat." Fitz stepped forward and touched her arm, gingerly, as if trying to soothe a skittish horse. "Maybe you and I and Kate should go somewhere and talk this out. Because really it's all my fault. I just couldn't resist—"

"Get off of me." Nat shook her arm free, her glare still fixed on Kate. "Ain't it sweet that your rich boyfriend wants to cover for you, huh, Katie? Guess you've really got him and his wallet wrapped around your finger."

"Nat!" Kate gasped, her face flaming. She didn't dare look

around at the others. But out of the corner of her eye, she could see Zara and Dani trading a look. Fitz was biting his lip, seeming at a loss for words for once. Summer was just staring with open curiosity.

Tommi cleared her throat. "Look, that's enough," she told Nat. "You don't know what you're—"

"Shut the hell up," Nat snapped. "I'm talking to Katie, not any of you rich bitches, okay?"

"Don't talk to her like that," Kate said. She meant it to sound stern, but the words came out weak and soft, flopping into the tense moment and just sort of lying there.

Nat stalked toward her. "You knew how much I was into this horse," she hissed. "And you stole him out from under me anyway. I was supposed to buy him, you know. Was already working out a deal with the Tanners."

"R-really?" Nat hadn't mentioned that before, and Kate wasn't sure whether to believe her. Why would she spend her hard-earned pennies buying a horse she could ride for free anytime she wanted?

Then again, why *wouldn't* she want to buy a horse like Flame? He was special—one in a million. Not that she'd imagined Nat realized it . . .

"Yeah, *really*," Nat spit out. "But you were just too jealous to let me keep him, weren't you? Couldn't stand to see me with a nicer horse than the overpriced dumbbloods at your fancy-schmancy barn." She waved a hand to encompass all of Pelham Lane. "So you sweet-talked Richie Rich here into snagging him out from under me."

"Hey," Fitz spoke up again. "That's not true. Kate didn't

even know I was buying him until he was already here. So if you're going to scratch someone's eyes out, it should be mine."

"Whatever." Nat's eyes flicked over to him before settling on Kate again. "Your girl made her choice, and she'll have to deal with it. So have a nice life, Katie. It's been real."

She spun on her heel and pushed past the others, banging into one of Dani's crutches on her way and practically knocking her over. A second later she was gone.

"Whoa," Zara breathed. "What the hell was *that*?"

Tommi stepped toward Kate from one direction and Fitz from the other. Both looked concerned.

"You all right, beautiful?" Fitz asked.

"Kate . . . ," Tommi began.

But Kate could feel her eyes filling with tears, and she knew that if she tried to speak they'd spill over. She'd had enough humiliation today; she didn't need to add to it.

Shaking her head, she turned and raced blindly down the aisle.

SIX

Ludlow Street was crowded and raucous, with blaring music pouring out of multiple storefronts—rock, hip-hop, alterna-weird. It was only ten o'clock, so there were still plenty of tourists and people walking their dogs mixing with the early-bird portion of the nighttime contingent, giving the entire block a strange sort of chaotic energy. The Middle Eastern restaurant around the corner emitted regular whiffs of exotic spices that hung in the humid air and tickled Tommi's nose as she stood in line outside the club where Alex was DJing that night.

"You okay?" Parker asked, nudging her in the side.

Tommi realized she hadn't heard anything her friends had said for the past five minutes. She'd shared a couple of cabs down here with Parker, Court, and their other friends James and Duckface.

"Huh?" she said, glancing at Parker. "Oh, yeah, fine. Just thinking."

"I know what she's thinking about," Court put in, tugging at the hem of her too-short minidress, which she'd bought on the shopping spree with Tommi the previous day. "She's still mad at me for tattling to Daddy about our trip down to Philly this weekend."

"Uh-oh, girl fight!" Duckface crowed, pumping his fist. A couple of college-age girls in line ahead of them glanced back at him over their Spandex-clad shoulders and giggled.

Tommi just rolled her eyes, not bothering to respond. Sure, she'd been a little annoyed with Court yesterday—but hadn't she maybe been secretly a little bit relieved, too? After all, it had taken the decision about whether to go or not out of her hands.

Anyway, it was done now. Once her father got an idea in his head, there was no changing his mind. And ever since Tommi had told him she wanted to become a horse pro after high school, he'd been determined to convince her of the value of a more traditional career path, which definitely started off with a college education. That meant Tommi was going to Penn this weekend, and that was that. No question, no guilt.

In any case, that wasn't what was distracting her right now. She was worrying about Kate. That had been quite a scene at the barn today. Tommi still couldn't believe Kate's so-called friend Natalie had crashed in like that and reamed her up one side and down the other in front of everyone. Even Fitz hadn't been able to cheer Kate up after that; she'd spent the rest of the afternoon moping around the barn, working even harder than usual.

"'Scuse me," Tommi mumbled to her friends. "I just need to make a quick call."

Stepping out of line, she found a relatively quiet spot in an apartment doorway and hit Kate's number on her phone. It rang four or five times, then went to voice mail.

"Damn," Tommi whispered, hanging up without leaving a message. She hoped Kate wasn't still at the barn. Okay, so it sounded like things were pretty tense for her at home. That didn't mean she needed to burn herself out working 24/7. At least she'd eaten the sandwich Tommi had brought her from the diner. That was something, anyway.

She rejoined her friends. "Everything okay?" James asked.

"Sure. Just checking in on a friend." Tommi heard someone calling her name. Glancing that way, she saw Alex winding through the crowd in their direction.

"You made it!" he exclaimed when he reached her, sounding breathless and happy and looking cuter than ever with his light brown eyes glittering with excitement and his slim torso encased in a vintage punk T-shirt.

"Wouldn't miss it." Tommi tipped her head back, letting her eyes fall shut briefly as he kissed her. She did her best to let her worries about Kate fall away. It wasn't as if she could do anything to help her right now, so she might as well enjoy the evening. "Someone who knows the DJ told me this is the place to be tonight."

Alex grinned. "Oh, yeah? I'm just here for the cute girls myself."

"Really? See any around here?" Parker pretended to peer off into the distance until Court punched him in the shoulder, which made Duckface and James laugh until they snorted.

"Don't pay any attention to them," Court told Alex. "We're all psyched to be here."

"Awesome. Thanks for coming, guys." Alex ran a hand through his spiky dark hair and glanced around at the crowd before his eyes came to rest on Tommi again. "Your friend Zara decide not to come?"

Tommi felt a twinge of annoyance. Alex was a huge Zac Trask fan. He'd been totally geeked when he'd found out that Zac's daughter rode at Tommi's barn. At first Tommi had thought it was kind of cute. After about the third time he'd buttonholed Zara and talked her ear off? Maybe not so cute anymore.

But hey, nobody was perfect, right? And one of the things she liked most about him was his serious passion for music. So she let it slide. Again.

"Nope, she couldn't make it," she said, not bothering to tell him that she hadn't even invited Zara tonight.

"Too bad." Alex shrugged and peered up and down the line again. "Looks like a pretty good crowd so far, though, huh?"

"Yeah." Duckface wriggled his skinny hips. "It going to be a par-tay!"

Court rolled her eyes. "Really?" she said. "*Par-tay*? What is this, nineteen eighty-five?"

Duckface just grinned and grabbed her, spinning her into a weird little square dance while Parker and James watched and cheered.

Tommi took advantage of their distraction to press up

against Alex and lower her voice. "So what song are you going to play for me tonight?" she murmured.

"Ah, ah, ah!" he scolded, grabbing her around the waist and pulling her toward him. "It's a surprise. You'll just have to wait and see."

"Hey, break it up!" Duckface said as Tommi and Alex kissed again. "Too much PDA."

Tommi couldn't help laughing, even in the middle of the kiss. That set Alex off, too, and they broke apart. "Guess I'd better get back in there," he said with a grin, reaching over to brush a strand of hair out of Tommi's face. "See you inside!"

"See you." Tommi smiled and tucked her hair behind one ear as she watched him race off. It was cool to see him in his element. This was what he wanted to do with his life—well, some version of it, anyway. He'd talked about being a pro-moter or band manager or various other things, but it was when the topic turned to his previous experiences DJing that he really came alive. And that made sense, actually. It was the perfect merging of his outgoing personality and his extensive and varied music collection. Up to now, the closest Tommi had come to seeing his skills firsthand was at that Hamptons house party, when Alex had kept them all entertained spin-ning tunes in the house, on the beach, and by the pool. But he'd kept getting interrupted by Court taking over to play some lame ballad or Duckface shorting out the speakers by dripping on them. So not really the same thing.

"Hey, if he's the DJ, how come we have to wait in line?" Parker complained. "We should get, like, VIP passes or some-thing!"

"Chill out." Court gave him a shove. "Line's already moving, see? We'll be inside sweating our asses off soon enough."

She was right. Within ten minutes they were inside the club, which was narrow and dark and smelled like stale beer. People were packed shoulder to shoulder by the bar and on the dance floor, and an old-school disco ball sent diamonds of light spinning around the room.

At the moment the sound system was playing a current pop hit called "Forgive Me" that seemed to be everywhere those days, from the jukebox at the diner near the barn to every station on Tommi's car radio. Tommi was already sick of it, but the chorus was so insanely catchy that she caught herself humming along:

"Forgive me/I know I done wrong/Forgive me, girl/'Cause I'm weak and you're strong . . ."

"Check it out," Court said as the song ended. "Loverboy's getting ready to start."

Tommi followed her gaze and saw that Alex had just stepped into the neon-striped DJ booth, which was set on a platform at one end of the long, narrow dance floor. He glanced out and spotted her, then grinned and waved and blew a kiss before returning his attention to the equipment.

"Aw, doesn't he look sexy up there, Tommi?" Duckface said into her ear.

"Shut up," Tommi said. But Duckface was right. Alex did look seriously cute, his expression intent as he focused on what he was doing.

"Drinks, anyone?" Parker asked.

Tommi followed her friends toward the bar. She had her

fake ID in her purse, but the bartender barely spared them a look as he asked what they were having. He was a big dude with a shaved head and a neck tattoo.

"Rum and Coke!" Court shouted at him. Then she glanced over her shoulder at Tommi. "Make it two?"

Tommi shook her head. "Just plain Coke for me," she said. "I have a lot to do tomorrow if we're leaving for Philly the next morning." That was true enough, though there was more to it than that. Tonight wasn't about partying. It was about seeing Alex do his thing. She didn't want to get wasted and miss out on even a little bit of that.

Court shrugged. "If you say so."

By the time they all made it back over to the edge of the dance floor, Alex was tapping his microphone. "You guys hear me?" he asked, his amplified voice floating over the crowd. "Welcome to my private music fantasy!"

"Whoo-hoo!" Duckface shouted, hoisting his beer over his head and sloshing half of it onto James and Parker in the process. "Gooooo, Nakano!"

Tommi laughed and let out a whistle. All around them, other people also whooped and cheered.

Alex grinned. "Cool, then let's get this party started," he said. "My name's Alex, and I'm basically the world's biggest music geek. I'm psyched to share my obsession with all of you tonight, okay, starting with a little band I discovered at this music festival in Boston and . . ."

"What's with telling us his life story?" Court said into Tommi's ear.

Tommi shrugged. Glancing around, she could see that

Court wasn't the only one wondering. All over the club, people were looking a little restless.

"Shut up and play some music!" someone shouted.

Alex didn't seem to hear; he rambled on for another minute or so about the remix he was about to play from an indie band. But finally he hit a button to send the first song blasting out through the speakers.

"Come on, let's dance!" Duckface was already boogying as he wriggled his way out onto the dance floor.

Court grabbed Tommi's hand and dragged her along. "Okay, this isn't exactly the song I'd choose to kick things off if I wanted people to dance," she said. "But hey, what do I know?"

Tommi felt a little self-conscious as she swayed to the beat with her friends. There were only a few other people out on the dance floor—some drunken frat-boy types, who kept jumping up and bumping chests with one another, laughing loudly the entire time; a heavily pierced couple slow dancing and making out; a lone Goth type who appeared to be having some kind of seizure.

James leaned closer. "Our boy's not exactly wowing the crowd, is he?" he said into Tommi's ear.

Tommi shrugged, glancing up at Alex. He was bent over his mixer, looking totally focused. "It's still early," Tommi told James. "I'm sure things will pick up."

But they didn't. An hour passed; Alex played a variety of songs and gave a few more of his little talks in between some of them. Tommi could tell from his voice and expression that he was genuinely geeked about the stuff he was saying. The trouble? Nobody else seemed to care. Whenever he started talking, everyone pretty much stampeded off the dance floor toward the bar—or the exit. By the time midnight rolled around, the club was less crowded than it had been when Tommi and her friends had arrived.

The worst part? Tommi wasn't sure Alex had even noticed. How was that possible? How could he *not* see that he was bombing? It sort of made her feel uncomfortable—and vaguely embarrassed for him.

As another song ended and Alex started blabbing about some vinyl-only music store he'd discovered in LA recently, Tommi grabbed Court and dragged her off the dance floor.

"I think I might take off," she said.

"Already? It's early."

Tommi shrugged. "Like I said, I've got a lot to do tomorrow," she said. "Tell Alex and the others I said good night, okay?"

Zara was fiddling with the TV remote when she heard the key scrape in the lock. A moment later her mother breezed in, looking flushed and happy and beautiful and maybe a little drunk. Her favorite diamond pendant sparkled against the jade green silk of her vintage Dior cocktail dress.

"You're still up!" Gina sang out, hurrying over to drop a kiss atop Zara's head. The scents of gin, smoke, and Chanel No. 5 floated around her.

"Hi," Zara said. "How was dinner?"

"Lovely. Stu and Evie are an absolute riot." Gina dropped her Fendi beaded clutch on the sofa and sank down next to it, graceful as a cat. Zara felt like reminding her that there was no camera there to record the performance, and nobody to see it except her. But she bit her tongue.

"That's good," she said instead. "By the way, before I forget, Stacie called while you were out."

"Oh?" Gina sat up straighter, suddenly looking more focused. "What do you mean, she called? I was hoping she'd still be up when I got home so we could finally get acquainted."

"Guess you'll have to wait a little longer." Zara shrugged, trying to look bored. "The interview dweebs loved her. They want her to stay for an extra day or two."

"Really." Gina's tone was even. When Zara chanced a quick glance, she found her mother gazing back at her. "Well, I suppose that's good news for her, isn't it?"

"Yeah, I guess." Zara could feel her palms starting to sweat. Her mother had been away for so long that Zara'd almost forgotten she had to be careful with her. She wasn't like Zac, who didn't really care if Zara lied to him as long as whatever she said didn't mess up his plans.

Then again, Zara was an experienced liar. She just had to get back in practice—like riding after a few weeks off. The muscles were a little soft and sore, but they still worked.

Good thing she hadn't tried to wing it. She'd spent most of the evening figuring out the best new excuse for Stacie's absence. For a while she'd thought about claiming that Stacie needed to stay at her "interview" for the entire rest of the week, but now she was glad she hadn't tried to push it. Gina already seemed a little suspicious. Zara would just have to figure out something new by Friday at the latest.

Gina stood, stretched, and wandered over to the wall of windows. Even at midnight, the sounds of whooshing traffic and blaring horns drifted up from the street below.

"It's nice to be back in New York," Gina said. "Always so much going on. Oh! That reminds me." She turned to face Zara. "There's a big movie premiere Friday night. The picture's just a talky thing about the Cold War or something, but the after-party should be fun. Want to be my date?"

Zara hesitated. Normally going to some boring industry function with her mom was the last thing she wanted to do on a perfectly good summer evening. But this time, maybe there was a reason to go.

"Um, sure, maybe." She stayed slouched on the sofa, keeping her voice and expression casual. "I mean, the movie sounds lame. But I might tag along if something better doesn't turn up."

"Wonderful!" Gina swept over and kissed her again. "Now I'd better get some beauty rest. Don't stay up too late, all right, love?"

"Sure, Mom. Good night." Zara waited until she heard her mother's door shut upstairs, then jumped to her feet and started pacing, thinking hard. This movie premiere? A stroke of luck. If she could keep herself and Gina out late enough on Friday night, that would buy her another day without having to worry about the Stacie thing. Then she just had to figure out how to handle the rest of the weekend until Gina flew out on Monday, and she was home free.

Kate kept her head down, staring at the TV remote in her lap. She'd taken her watch off when she'd showered after coming home from the barn earlier, but she knew exactly what time it was. Or at least what time it had been when Andy had strolled in a few minutes ago. Twelve twenty-three. More than an hour past his new curfew. Her father wasn't about to let Andy forget it.

Or Kate, either, since she was trapped here listening to the two of them argue. Unless she wanted to squeeze between them to get to the stairs, that was. And there was no way she was doing that.

She sneaked a look at her mother, who was curled into a quivering ball of neurosis on the easy chair nearby. Great. If this didn't set Mom off on one of her serious OCD sprees, it would be a miracle. She'd been getting bad even before this—not that Andy seemed to care.

Kate shot her younger brother a look, feeling a flash of anger toward him. Why couldn't he just be normal? Go back to being the smiling, sweet-natured kid he'd been up until this year?

Hearing a light tapping sound, Kate glanced at her mother again. There she went. *Tap, tap, tap, tap.* Four quick taps on the arm of the chair. Exactly four. Always four. What was it about that number that made it so damn magical in her mother's head, anyway? Kate tried not to think about it.

"I wouldn't have to sneak around if you weren't such a freaking unreasonable hardass!" Andy was yelling at their father. "None of my friends have to be home so early!"

"That's because your friends are losers," Kate's father retorted.

Tap, tap, tap, tap. Pause. *Tap, tap, tap, tap.*

Kate gritted her teeth, trying not to count along. "Listen, Andy," she spoke up, sick and tired of her brother acting like such a brat. "Just calm down, okay? Lots of kids your age have curfews, and Dad is only—"

"Shut the hell up!" Andy whirled on her, his expression hostile. "What the hell do you know about anything, you dumb bitch?"

"Andrew! Language!" their mother gasped out, just as her husband exploded in a torrent of curses.

But Kate couldn't respond at all. This was just too much. She couldn't stand it anymore; couldn't spend one more second in this house. If she did, she'd go crazy herself. Feeling her eyes fill with tears, she dropped the remote and rushed for the door, grabbing her car keys off the fussy little fake-cast-iron key hook on the way.

"Katie?" she heard her father call after her.

Her hands didn't stop shaking until her car was three blocks away. She drifted to a stop in the middle of the street; no big deal, since there was no other traffic in sight. Aside from the blue-green glow of a TV through a window here and there and the rumble of Kate's car's engine, the entire neighborhood was dark and silent.

She clutched the steering wheel, realizing she had no idea where she was going. Normally at a time like this she'd run to Nat, but that was obviously out of the question.

The barn? For a second her foot touched the gas pedal, ready to follow the familiar route to Pelham Lane. This time of night, with no traffic, she could be there in five minutes.

Then she shook her head. She didn't dare go there right now, either. Jamie had already talked to her about working too hard, spending too much time at the barn. Besides, he was big on family. He'd want her to go home and work things out with her parents.

Reaching for her phone, she scrolled through until she came to Tommi's number. Tommi had told her she had her back, no matter what. Was it time to put that to the test?

She hit the number and waited. Two rings. Three. Four . . .

When Tommi's voice mail message started, Kate hung up, feeling tears well up again. But she blinked them away and hit the next number on her list.

This time, it only took one ring. "Hey, gorgeous," Fitz said. "What's up?"

"N-nothing." Kate sniffled, unreasonably happy to hear his voice sounding so normal. "What are you doing?"

"Playing video games all by myself. Totally boring and pathetic." He paused as she sniffled again. "Hey, what's wrong? You sound weird. Is everything okay?"

"Yes. I mean no. I mean, not really . . ." Kate's voice quavered, but she didn't care. Suddenly she couldn't keep it in anymore, couldn't pretend everything was all right. And he was supposed to care about her, right? So she told him the whole story.

"Oh, man," Fitz said when she'd finished. "Want me to come out and beat up your brat of a brother for you?"

Kate couldn't help smiling. "No, that's okay," she said. "He's not a bad kid, really. I mean, he doesn't mean to be. He's just going through some stuff right now, and our dad really is kind of inflexible sometimes. . . . I just needed to get away from the whole thing for a while."

"Gotcha. Okay, then, why don't you come crash here for tonight?"

She blinked. "What?"

"You probably just have to time to make it to Chappaqua and grab the last train out," Fitz said. "I'll pick you up at Grand Central. Or hell, if you miss the train I'll drive out and get you."

Kate didn't answer for a second, actually sort of tempted. But then the more rational part of her mind took over. Leave it to Fitz to come up with a sweet yet crazy plan like that. But it was late, and she had to be at the barn bright and early tomorrow for work. Commuting in and out of the city just because she wanted to get away from her crazy family? Not exactly practical. Besides, just talking to Fitz, letting it out, had made her feel a lot calmer already.

"Thanks," she said, meaning it. "But that's okay. I just needed to vent to someone, I guess."

"You sure?" Fitz sounded unconvinced.

"Yeah. Seriously, thanks. I'll see you tomorrow, okay?"

"Okay. Just call again if you need to. Anytime."

After Kate hung up, she just sat there for a moment staring out at the night, her brain in neutral. But finally she put the car into gear and drove home, sneaking in the back door so she didn't have to face her family.

Tommi was yawning when she stepped into the brownstone, trying to decide if she had the energy for a shower or if it could wait until morning. Someone had left the front hall light on for her, and she noticed another light glowing out from beyond the kitchen in the back—it was coming from her father's home office. A moment later he appeared at the end of the hall in sweats, his tattered old robe, and a baseball cap.

"Tommi," he said, checking his watch. "Thought I'd be waiting up a lot later than this for you tonight."

"Hi, Dad." Tommi kicked off her shoes and picked them up, then headed for the stairs. "I told you a million times, you don't have to wait up for me. You know I'd call if I ran into any trouble."

"I know." He walked over and put an arm around her shoulders, giving her a quick hug. "But I feel better when I know you're home. Besides, I had some paperwork to catch up on."

"Okay." Stifling another yawn, Tommi continued toward the staircase. "Anyway, I'm beat. See you in the morning."

"Hang on." He waited until Tommi turned to face him again. "Listen, Tommi. I just wanted to tell you how glad I was to hear about this trip down to Penn this weekend. It's good that you're keeping all your options open. Sign of maturity— I'm proud of you."

"Um, thanks." He was obviously reading a lot more into this road trip than was really there, but Tommi didn't feel like getting into it right then. Let him think what he wanted. Maybe it would keep him off her back for a while about Legs, anyway. "Good night, Dad."

She plodded up the stairs, trying not to think about Alex. She just wanted to fall into bed and forget this whole evening had ever happened. But what was she supposed to say to him when he asked what she'd thought of his DJing? Suddenly she couldn't help being very glad she was getting out of town for a while.

SEVEN

— — — — —

"So Joy told me she thinks she knows someone who has a really cool carriage, kind of like the one in, like, *Cinderella* or something. Really elegant, you know? Only I need for her to make sure the horses they use are either white or black. I mean, how ridic would it be if they turned up with, like, some bright orangey chestnuts or something? Talk about mortifying!"

Kate glanced over as Summer paused, seeming to expect a response. "Um, what?"

"Chestnut horses. My pink dress? Total fashion faux pas, right?" Summer paused again. When Kate didn't say anything, Summer's brow crinkled into an impatient frown. "What's wrong with you?" she complained. "It's like you're not even paying attention to anything I'm saying!"

"Sorry," Kate mumbled, stifling a yawn. She so wasn't in the mood for Summer right now. The girl had been following her around the barn for the past hour—at least it *felt* like that long—bragging about her over-the-top party plans. At the moment she was leaning against the tack room wall, watching Kate clean Jamie's training bridles.

"Anyway," Summer went on, "did I tell you how idiotic my mom is being about the ice sculpture? I thought we'd agreed to make it a life-size horse and rider—based on me, of course—but now she's trying to talk me into turning it into some kind of sushi pyramid instead. How lame is that? I don't even like sushi!"

Kate was relieved to see Marissa enter. Maybe Summer would latch on to her for a while and leave Kate alone. Marissa was good-natured enough to tolerate Summer—she even seemed to like her most of the time—and might actually care about stuff like Summer's fancy pink dress and her sushi-shaped ice sculpture.

"Hey, guys," Marissa greeted them, pushing her springy brown hair out of her face. "Summer, Miguel's looking for you. I guess Whiskey is in the indoor ring, barking and spooking the ponies in the little kids' lesson. You're supposed to come get him before Jamie feeds him to one of the bigger dogs."

Summer rolled her eyes. "Seriously? How hard is it to shoo a dog out of the ring?"

Still, she hurried out of the room. Marissa glanced at the set of reins Kate was wiping down. "Need any help with that?"

"Thanks, but I'm almost done." Kate swiftly figure-eighted the bridle and hung it up, brushing a few smears of neatsfoot oil off on her jeans. "Hey, have you seen Tommi around?"

Marissa shook her head. "I thought she wasn't coming up today? She said something yesterday about going away for the weekend or something."

"Oh, yeah, I forgot." Kate's heart sank as she realized Marissa was right. She'd been so focused on needing to talk to Tommi that she'd completely forgotten about that weekend trip, even though Tommi had told her all about it while they were hosing down some horses together the day before.

Out of the corner of her eye, she watched Marissa reach up and redo the clip that was holding her hair in a big, poofy ponytail.

"Don't stare at my frizz," Marissa said with a grimace. "I swear, if it gets any hotter all the bobby pins and hairspray in the world won't keep my hair under my helmet while I ride."

"Your hair always looks good," Kate said, feeling distracted. "Much better than my limp and stringy mess." She ran one hand over her long, blond ponytail.

Marissa peered at her. "You okay? You look kind of, I don't know, worried or something."

Kate quickly forced a smile. Sometimes it was easy to forget that Marissa didn't miss much. She might seem kind of ditzy, blabbing about hair and boys and stuff, but she really wasn't. "I'm fine," Kate said. "Just tons to do, as usual."

Sure, she was trying to be more open with Tommi these days. Let her in, let her help. But she and Marissa weren't *that* kind of friends. No way could she talk to her about her family problems. Not unless she wanted it broadcast all over the greater New York metro. Marissa meant well, but she didn't always think before she gossiped.

"Um, how's Dani doing?" Kate asked instead. "Have you talked to her?"

"Yeah, I called her this morning. She's doing fine, but she

misses all of us like crazy. She's hoping she can talk her older brother into driving her out here soon for another visit." Marissa grinned. "In the meantime, I'm making sure to keep her up to date on all the barn gossip."

Kate smiled back weakly. "That's good." She quickly tossed her tack cleaning supplies back into the cupboard. "Anyway, I'd better go bring in the rest of the mares before the flies start to drive them cr—"

Before she could finish, Fitz burst into the tack room. "Good, you're here," he said, hurrying over and dropping a kiss on Kate's lips.

Marissa giggled. "What am I, chopped liver?"

"I'm glad you're here, too, Miss Rissa." Fitz stepped over and planted a loud smooch on her forehead. "Forgive me?"

"How can any woman resist your charms?" Marissa smirked. "But I'll leave you two alone now. I know when I'm in the way." With a broad wink, she hurried out of the room.

Fitz wrapped his arms around Kate's waist. "Good morning," he said softly, then bent and kissed her again. "You okay?"

Kate smiled up at him gratefully. "Yeah, mostly. Thanks for listening last night."

"Anytime." He ran his finger along her face, tracing the line of her jaw. "I'm always here for you, Kate." Then he smiled. "Hey, I know something that'll take your mind off of everything. How about another session with Flame?"

Kate felt a little flutter of anticipation. She'd been so distracted by everything else that she hadn't had much time to think about yesterday's ride on the chestnut gelding. But suddenly her mind was filled with him, and she couldn't wait to ride him again.

"Um, okay," she told Fitz. "Can you start tacking up without me? I just need to bring in some horses first."

A few minutes later she was swinging into the saddle. The big outdoor ring was deserted—it was already an oven outside, and Jamie had moved his lessons into the shady indoor with its industrial overhead fans. Despite the heat and humidity, Flame was moving forward easily, seeming eager to work.

"Good boy," Kate said softly as she sent him into a walk. She quickly reviewed what they'd done yesterday as she warmed him up—transitions, some baby lateral work, just the basics to start teaching him what her leg aids meant.

By the time they started cantering, Kate was smiling from ear to ear. Sure, Flame made a mistake here and there—jumped into a canter when she wanted him to extend his trot, cut the corners to avoid bending, minor stuff like that. But he was trying, and learning faster than any horse she'd ridden in a long time. After nailing his second canter depart in a row, she brought him back to a walk and gave him a rub on the neck.

"You're a superstar," she murmured. "Such a good, good boy."

"Should I set up a couple of jumps?" Fitz was already moving toward the pile of poles and standards at one end of the ring. "See what we've got? I can text Jamie and make sure he's okay with it."

Kate hesitated, tempted. Based on the way this horse moved, she was pretty sure he was going to be a naturally talented jumper. She was dying to find out for sure.

But she shook her head. "Not this time," she told Fitz. "This horse was on the track like a month ago, remember? Whoever started him for racing obviously gave him some good basic

— 92 —

training, but he still needs to learn a ton of stuff for his new job. We don't want to rush him and fry his mind."

"You sure?" Fitz sounded disappointed. "But maybe just a crossrail or two, see if he's got the instincts . . ."

"Sorry." Kate ran her fingers through the horse's mane, then gave him another pat. "I just think it's better to wait."

Fitz frowned, and for a second Kate thought he was going to argue. Then he shrugged. "Okay, you're the boss. We'll wait until you think he's ready."

Kate nodded and sent Flame into an easy trot again, doing a few big, loopy circles and other figures. She was glad Fitz hadn't pushed harder to move faster. Flame was a quick learner and probably would have been fine, but Kate couldn't help remembering how tense and confused he'd been at that little show where they'd seen Nat ride him. That kind of ham-handed riding could ruin even the nicest horse.

She immediately felt guilty for the thought. But she did her best not to worry about it. Clucking softly, she sent Flame into another canter and let all thoughts of Nat—and everything else—drift away.

Tommi parked her red leather roller bag on the curb and glanced up and down the block. It was early, but the leafy shade of the gingko trees lining the street in front of the brownstone offered little relief from the stifling heat already settling over the city.

She felt her phone vibrate in her shorts pocket and pulled it out. It was a text from Alex:

have fun in philly—but not 2 much! lol. miss u already.

Tommi tucked the phone away again without answering. She hadn't actually spoken to Alex since leaving the club the other night, though she'd texted to invite him to Summer's party, and they'd traded a few more texts after that. Light and breezy, typical text stuff, so not too hard to imply that she'd had a good time without actually coming out and saying it. Not that she was afraid of a little white lie to save someone's feelings, of course. But this time it just felt different somehow . . .

A blaring car horn interrupted her thoughts, sending her involuntarily jumping back away from the curb. A second later she heard a shout of laughter.

The car, a bright red Audi convertible with the top down, screeched to a halt, double-parking a few car lengths down the street. A pop song was blasting out of the speakers, and three girls were grinning at her.

"Gotcha, Aaronson!" Abby waved from the driver's seat. She was Tommi's age and height but probably outweighed her by thirty pounds, though not because she was fat. Abby's friends sometimes called her Earth Mama because she was built like one of those pagan fertility goddesses—all boobs, hips, and thighs. In middle school Abby had tried to fight those endowments with strict diets and too-tight clothes, but a couple of years ago she'd embraced her natural look by dressing in flowing boho dresses and allowing her mass of curly-wavy brown hair to fly free. It worked for her, though her gorgeous chocolate-drop eyes and easygoing, fun-loving personality helped, too.

Tommi smiled and rolled her eyes, grabbing the handle of her bag and heading toward the car. "You're sooo funny, Abs."

Brooke jumped out of the passenger seat and rushed over to give Tommi a hug. She was tall and slim and changed the color of her pixie-cut hair so often that Tommi couldn't remember its original shade. Today it was platinum blond with a dramatic electric blue stripe that matched the metallic threads in her retro babydoll sundress.

"Glad you could make it," she told Tommi. Then she hurried around to open the trunk. "See if you can fit your stuff in here. But good luck. Court packed, like, her entire wardrobe."

"Hey, you never know what's going to appeal to college boys. I want to be prepared." Court was in the backseat, relaxing with one arm hanging over the side door. She looked cool and elegant in beige linen, oversize Burberry shades covering half her face.

Tommi shoved her bags in with her friends' luggage and slammed the trunk shut. "Good thing you picked me up before Mariah," she said as she slid into the backseat beside Court. The car was supposed to seat five, but it was a tight squeeze. "She always brings even more stuff than Court."

"Yeah. And a really good thing Brooke shipped most of her stuff down to Penn last week," Court said. "Otherwise we'd be making this trip in a moving van instead of Ab's car."

Abby was back in the driver's seat by then. She revved the engine. "Philadelphia, here we come!" she cried.

"Don't you mean Eighty-First Street, here we come?" Brooke said.

"Whatev. It's all in the same direction." Abby pulled out, cutting off a cab that blared loudly in response.

Court lifted one hand and flipped the driver the bird. "So

when we get down there, should we—oh, hey, crank it up!" she interrupted herself as a new song came on the radio.

"'Forgive Me'? Ugh, are you serious?" Brooke groaned. "They only play it, like, ten million times per hour!"

Court ignored her, singing along loudly as Abby steered the car onto Lexington Avenue. Brooke shrugged and joined in, waving both hands over her head in time to the music.

Tommi smiled, feeling some of their giddiness rubbing off on her. This trip should be fun, even if Tommi hadn't been sure about going. So what if her father was reading too much into it? She'd already decided on her life plan, and it didn't involve moving onto some college campus in another city. He'd just have to deal with that.

Soon the car was pulling to a stop in front of Mariah's high-rise building. Mariah was waiting outside, looking impatient. She was into the old-school preppy look these days, and was rocking it in madras shorts and a monogrammed polo, her halo of tight black curls tamed by a matching headband. She rushed toward the car as her doorman followed with her bags.

"Oh my God, you guys, this is going to be so fun!" she exclaimed. Her eyes lit up when she saw Tommi. "Wow, so they actually talked you into coming? I can't believe it! I thought you were pretty much chained to that barn of yours."

"She's here," Abby confirmed with a grin. "And she doesn't even smell like horses for once."

"Good thing," Court put in. "I hear cute Cousin Jon isn't into animals, if you know what I mean."

While Tommi gave Court a playful punch on the arm,

Brooke pretended to pout. "Hey, I'm starting to think you guys are only coming for my allegedly hot cousin, not for me."

"There's no allegedly about it. He's hot with a capital H.O.T." Court fanned herself with one hand.

"Whatever. Get in and let's get moving. I want to get there before lunchtime." Abby revved the engine.

Tommi leaned back against her seat, enjoying the occasional bursts of air against her face as the convertible threaded its way through the city. Yes, she was looking forward to this trip—if only to get some space to figure out why that night at the club was still bugging her so much. So Alex hadn't exactly lit the crowd on fire. So what? It was probably like riding. Blowing one class—or even one show—didn't mean it was time to trade your spurs for a tennis racket.

The difference? She always knew when she'd blown a class. And Alex seemed totally clueless about how he'd really done. One of the things she'd liked most about him from the start was his passion for music. She'd seen it as a big thing they had in common—he was committed to finding a way to make music the focus of his life, just like she was with the horses.

But now it seemed that at least one of them might be deluded in thinking he could actually turn that passion into a real career. What if it was *both* of them?

"Aaaaah!" Brooke yelled as Abby turned left onto Ninth Avenue, almost sideswiping a delivery truck.

Abby just grinned, gunning the motor to pass a slow-moving car. "And the adventure begins," she intoned.

Tommi laughed, putting all thoughts of Alex's career issues out of her mind. While she was at it, she vowed not to worry about her own future, either. Or how she was going to sell Legs in time. Or anything else that could get in the way of her fun.

Because yeah. This should be an adventure, all right. Why not forget about real life for one weekend and just go with it?

*

"You look gorgeous, my love." Gina smiled, looking Zara up and down. "Positively stunning!"

Zara glanced at her reflection in the mirrored side wall of the foyer. She really did look pretty hot, all dolled up in a semi-sheer black minidress and strappy Manolo heels. Her hair was slicked back and up from her face, but it was loose on top, allowing her natural curls to go wild.

"Thanks." Zara didn't bother to return the compliment. Gina didn't need anyone to tell her she was beautiful—she'd made her living off of it for the past twenty years. Everyone at the premiere would probably fall all over themselves drooling over her one-shouldered white gown, her upswept 'do, the dangling diamond earrings sparkling against her flawless dark skin. Blah, blah, blah.

Gina grabbed her clutch off the console in the message center, pausing to glance at the answering machine. The little glowing screen was blank. No messages.

"Too bad Stacie hasn't made it back yet," Gina said. "She could have tagged along, too."

Zara leaned toward the mirror, avoiding her mother's eye while pretending to check her makeup. "Yeah," she said. "Uh, she sent me a text a little while ago saying the train station was crazy and not to wait for her. You know how it is on Friday nights—half of New Jersey is trying to cram itself across the bridges and tunnels to come party in Manhattan."

"That's what I hear." Gina glanced in the mirror herself, then headed for the door. "I suppose we'd better go, then."

They headed for the elevator. The loft was only five stories up, and Zara often took the stairs down, but no way was she going to suggest that tonight. For one thing, her mother's Louboutins were even higher than her own heels. Besides, she was counting on that elevator to help her with the latest step in her plan.

Zara started digging through her purse while they waited. As soon as the bell dinged, indicating that the elevator was here, she let out a snort. "Oh, man," she said as the old-fashioned door wheezed open and her mother stepped inside. "Forgot my lipstick. See you downstairs?"

"Sure," her mother replied. "I'll meet you at the car."

As the elevator door slid shut, Zara breathed out a sigh. It had worked.

Hurrying back into the loft, she made a beeline for the guest room upstairs. She pulled out the rumpled jeans she'd hidden under the bed earlier, draping them over a chair. She'd stuck a couple of spare pillows from the linen closet under there, too. Yanking them out, she pulled back the sheets and arranged the pillows carefully, then pulled the sheets back over them and stepped back to survey the result. Yeah, it kind of looked like a sleeping body. At least it would if it was dark in the room and whoever was looking was a little tipsy.

Then Zara remembered the final touch. Hurrying over to the dresser, she opened the top drawer. She'd stashed one of

Zac's old wigs in there. Okay, so it was kind of a light brown, while Stacie was more of a dishwater blond. Close enough, especially since Gina wouldn't know the difference. Zara tucked the wig under the covers, leaving just a hint of hair spilling out. Perfect.

"This is so lame-ass Disney Channel," she muttered as she tweaked the wig so a little more of it showed.

But what choice did she have?

She turned to go before her mother got suspicious. This time she bypassed the slow elevator, kicking off her high-heeled sandals and taking the stairs in her bare feet. Halfway down her phone buzzed. She pulled it out, wondering if it was Gina getting impatient.

But it wasn't. It was a text from Grant.

everything ok, beautiful? haven't heard from u in a while. are u getting my texts? need to see u soon or I'll go crazy!

"Give me a freaking break," she muttered. She so wasn't in the mood to deal with Mr. Needy right now. Or really ever, come to think of it.

Slinging the straps of her sandals over one wrist, she quickly typed a response.

rly busy right now. its been fun, but I'm not right for u. we should see other people.

She sent the message, then dropped her phone back in her purse and ran down the rest of the steps two at a time.

EIGHT

———————

"Want another soda?"

Tommi smiled up at Cousin Jon from her spot on the world's lumpiest sofa. He was almost as cute as Court had promised, with tousled blond hair that just touched the collar of his T-shirt, and bright blue eyes with a hint of mischief.

"No thanks, I'm good," Tommi told him. "Anyway, aren't we going out to eat soon?"

Jon's housemate, Rashad, looked over and chuckled. "Maybe if your friend ever makes it out of the bathroom," he said. "Hope the roaches didn't get her."

"Ew!" Court wrinkled her nose and glanced around with a look of slight distaste. They'd all been hanging out at the guys' off-campus house since the girls had arrived, talking and getting acquainted. The place was pretty much a dump, with thrift-shop furniture and ratty linoleum. The sofa Tommi, Rashad, and Court were sitting on smelled faintly of beer and puke.

But it was supposed to be an adventure, right? Tommi was trying to keep that in mind. Besides, the important thing was that there was plenty of room for all of them to stay, since the other housemates weren't coming back to campus until the following weekend. It didn't hurt that both Jon and Rashad were so easy on the eyes, either. Rashad was tall and built like an athlete, which made sense, since he'd already mentioned he was on the university's rugby team. He had short dreads, a pierced brow, and an easy grin.

"So what are we doing tonight, anyway?" Mariah bounced up and down on the edge of a rickety-looking wooden chair. "I mean, dinner first, obviously. I'm starving. But what about after?"

The two guys exchanged a glance. "One of the frats is having their annual So Long Summer party tonight," Cousin Jon said. "Thought we might hit that up, if you're into it."

"Sounds like a plan." Brooke was perched on another chair, picking at her fingernails. "Think it'll be fun?"

Cousin Jon nodded. "For sure. Those guys know how to throw a party. This one time last year . . ."

He launched into a story about some epic past party. A funny one, if the reactions from Tommi's friends were any indication.

But Tommi couldn't seem to focus. Her mind was wandering northward—back to Pelham Lane, to be exact. Was Kate still at the barn, working away another Friday night? Had she eaten? And how had Joy's schooling session with Legs gone? Had he behaved himself?

She blinked and glanced up as Abby appeared in the

doorway, bringing with her a cloud of her signature gardenia scent. "All ready," Abby sang out, dropping her lip gloss into her hobo bag. "Let's go have some fun!"

"Food first, then fun," Brooke said.

Rashad jumped to his feet and held out a hand to help Tommi up. "So you ever been to a frat party?"

"Nope. Frat virgin here," Tommi responded lightly as she took his hand. "Should be an adventure."

"For sure." He squeezed her hand and smiled. His palm felt warm and dry, and as Tommi smiled back, she suddenly found herself having a lot less trouble focusing on the here and now.

Zara took a deep breath, then climbed out of the limo after her mother. Flashes went off from every direction, making it hard to see, but she kept her eyes focused on Gina's white dress just ahead.

"Gina! Gina!" a dozen voices shouted. The crowd surged forward, pressing against the ropes blocking off a narrow pathway across the sidewalk and into the theater.

Gina stopped and struck a pose, shooting her most dazzling smile at the paparazzi. After a moment she turned and beckoned to Zara.

Zara almost rolled her eyes, then remembered that someone would be sure to capture it on film for all to see. So she pasted a bored little smile on her face and stepped toward her mother, willing herself not to trip over her high heels. Gina grabbed her hand and pulled her in close.

"Smile, my love," she whispered without moving her lips.

A thousand more flashes, and finally they moved on. Zara's heart was beating fast as they ducked into the theater lobby; that was the first red carpet she'd walked since moving to New York. And yeah, she had to admit she'd missed it. At least a little. The adrenaline rush, the dangerous feeling that one wrong move could plaster her on the front of tabloids all over the world. Or one right move, depending how you looked at it. She'd had some fun with that sort of thing in the past, but tonight wasn't the time.

"Gina, darling!" A painfully skinny red-haired woman rushed toward them. Zara recognized her as one of Gina's costars from a previous film, an over-the-hill boozy-floozy type who'd seen a few tabloid covers herself.

As the two actresses made kissy-face at each other, Zara stepped away and surveyed the lobby. It was all decked out in red and gray bunting—something to do with the topic of the movie, she guessed. There was a bar set up beside the snack stand, and several people were standing in front of it sipping martinis and looking self-important. Then a well-known action star entered, and everyone turned to stare at him.

"Same crap, different coast," Zara said under her breath. It had become one of her favorite sayings since moving to New York. She glanced around for her mother, but Gina had disappeared somewhere in the rapidly swelling crowd.

Zara sauntered over to the bar. "Hey," she said to the bartender, a harried-looking middle-aged woman in a too-tight black-and-white uniform. "Tequila slammer, please."

The woman squinted at her. "Are you—" she began.

"Zara! Gorgeous girl!" a loud, high-pitched voice exclaimed.

Zara winced. She turned to face the woman, a successful character actress who'd been in practically every movie and TV show for the past three decades as far as Zara could tell. She'd lived right across the street from them back in Hollywood.

"Hi, Camille," Zara said. "Are you in this movie?"

"Just a tiny part, sadly." Camille waved a hand and tittered. "Barely a cameo. But never mind that, how are you, sweetheart? How's school? What will you be this year—a junior, yes?"

Zara shot a look at the bartender. So much for that.

"Yeah," she said. "Um, but school doesn't start for a few more weeks."

She continued to chitchat with Camille until they were interrupted by some fast-talking skinny dude in a suit. Zara took the opportunity to escape, ducking behind a potted palm to avoid pushing through the mob.

When she emerged on the other side, she almost crashed into a guy standing off by himself, staring out into the crowd. She stopped short, but couldn't quite avoid stepping on his heel.

"Oops," she blurted out. "Sorry."

He turned to face her. "No worries," he said, his husky voice betraying a slight twang.

Zara blinked and lifted one eyebrow as she checked him out. Okay, this was more like it. The guy was probably four or five years older than her and crazy hot. Strong chin, two or three days' stubble, shaggy dark hair that looked like it had never seen a comb. Wearing a vintage leather jacket despite the heat outside. He was a little unkempt. Maybe a little dangerous. In other words, just her type.

"I'm Zara," she said. "You come here often?"

He smiled, which made the corners of his eyes crinkle and revealed a slight dimple in one cheek. Nice.

"Constantly. I'm addicted to popcorn grease," he responded. "You?"

Just then Gina appeared again. She shot a quick, distracted smile at the guy, then took Zara by the arm. "Shall we go in, love?" she said. "The film should be starting soon."

"Yeah," the guy said. "See you, Zara."

"Who was that?" Gina asked as he drifted off through the crowd.

"Um . . ." Zara realized she hadn't gotten his name. "Just some guy. Come on, let's go in."

An hour later, Zara stifled another yawn. The film was super boring—just a bunch of guys with slicked-back hair and dark suits talking urgently at one another and pounding their fists on desks. Zara leaned toward her mother.

"I'm hitting the bathroom," she whispered.

She slid out of her seat and hurried up the aisle. Maybe she could snag some food to pass the time until the after-party—or if she was lucky, a drink.

The lobby was a lot less crowded than before, though there were still a few people out there. Zara scanned the stragglers with a practiced eye. The woman with the frosted hair and the spray-on tan yapping into her cell phone was probably an agent or publicist trying to drum up some extra media attention for whichever client of hers was inside right now. The fat guy leaning on the bar flirting with the bartender? Definitely an aspiring producer. Zara knew the type.

Then she felt someone staring and turned around. It was Mr. Leather Jacket.

He was already moving toward her, slouched with hands in pockets. "Hey," he said when he was close enough.

"Hey yourself." Zara tilted her head and hinted at a smile. Yeah, he was just as hot as she'd thought the first time. "Boring movie, huh?"

"Uh-huh, kinda." The guy shrugged. "It's not really my type of flick, but some friends dragged me along." She could tell he was trying not to stare at her cleavage. His eyes flickered down a couple of times, but he was doing pretty well considering how low-cut her dress was. "So how come you're here?" he added.

Zara was a little surprised. Didn't the guy know who she was? Didn't he know who *Gina* was? He had to be either blind or faking. And when she saw those dark brown eyes slip downward again, she was pretty sure he wasn't blind.

"Uh, my mom talked me into coming," Zara said. "Guess I'm her date, since my dad's out of town."

"Cool." He glanced toward the bar. "I was hoping to grab a beer or something, but I got carded."

Again, surprise. Zara would've guessed he was at least twenty-one, if not a year or two older. "Really? How old are you?" she asked.

A smile played over his lips. "Isn't that kind of a personal question? Like, a lady never reveals her age or whatever?"

"Are you a lady?" Zara shot back. "Because if you are, you need to invest in some serious waxing."

He laughed. "If you must know, I'm twenty. What about you? Or are you going to turn that lady thing back on me now?"

"Don't worry, I'm no lady." Zara smirked. "Sixteen. Almost seventeen."

"Jailbait. Nice." He grinned. "So Zara, are you—"

"Excuse me." A middle-aged man bustled over and got in their faces. "We're going to start filming some interviews out here in just a moment, so I have to ask you to head back into the theater now, all right?"

Zara frowned, about to tell the guy off. But Mr. Leather Jacket was nodding. "No problem, bro," he said. "After you, Zara."

He stepped over and held the door. Zara couldn't remember the last time a guy had actually held a door for her, old-school gentlemanly like that. Well, except maybe Mickey from her dad's posse. Or some of the newer lackeys when they wanted to suck up. But they didn't count.

She wasn't sure how to react, other than to nod and step past into the darkened theater. On the screen, some chiseled dude in a tux was lighting a cigarette. The flare of the match distracted her for a moment; then she felt Mr. Leather Jacket touch her lightly on the arm as he brushed past her. He hurried forward and disappeared into one of the rows up front.

Zara just stood there for a few seconds as her brain caught up. Then she frowned.

"Dammit!" she said out loud, earning annoyed glances from the people in nearby seats. She *still* didn't know the guy's name.

Kate had barely slipped her key into the lock when the door swept open. "It's about time you—oh, Katie." Her father's shoulders slumped, and his loud voice softened. "Uh, come on in."

"What's going on?" Kate stepped inside, glancing from her father to her mother, who was over by the fireplace dusting the candlesticks with a rag. One, two, three, four candlesticks . . . Kate winced and looked back at her dad.

He looked tired as he passed one hand over his face. "It's your brother," he said gruffly. "He picked a fight with your mother earlier and ran out in a huff. Now he won't answer his phone."

Kate closed her eyes for a second. So they were in for another long night of drama. After her busy day at the barn, she wasn't sure she could handle that.

"Um, I just remembered," she said. "I left, uh, something in my car."

She darted out and closed the door behind herself without waiting for an answer. Her heart was pounding, and the chicken wrap she'd eaten earlier was popcorning around in her stomach. She couldn't do this. Not tonight. If she had to stay here for another installment of Psycho Family Drama Night, she'd go crazy. For real.

But what other choice did she have? Where could she go?

Nat was still out, obviously. Kate hadn't heard a peep out of her since that day at Pelham Lane. Talk about drama . . .

She shoved aside all thoughts of Nat. Tommi? Kate was pretty sure she'd let her crash at her place in the city, even if Kate would feel totally awkward about it. But that wasn't an option right now, either, since Tommi had left for Philadelphia that morning.

Okay, so what about Fitz? He was on his own with his parents out of the country, and he was always up for a night out. Maybe she could convince him to come up, hang out with her at the diner or somewhere until it was late enough for her parents to be asleep.

Not letting herself stop to think, she dialed his number. He answered on the second ring.

"Kate?" he said. "Everything okay?"

"What, can't I just call to say hi?" she tried to joke, though her voice came out a little wobbly.

"*Are* you just calling to say hi?"

"Not exactly . . ." She told him what was going on. "So I was thinking, if you wanted to come up and—"

"I'll be there as soon as I can get there," Fitz interrupted. "Pack a few things; you can stay here as long as you need to."

"What?" Kate blurted out, startled. "Um, no, I just meant—"

"What's your address again? I can pick you up in front of your place."

"No!" Kate swallowed hard. "I mean, I can meet you at the barn, okay? It's closer."

"Fine. See you there in a while."

The phone clicked to dead air. Kate stared at it. Running

away to stay with Nat or Tommi for a night or two was one thing. But she couldn't, like, *move in* with her boyfriend. No way. That was crazy. Right?

She headed toward the house, her thumb hovering over the button to call him back. As she swung open the door, her father's voice drifted out from the direction of the kitchen, sounding angry. He was yelling at Kate's mother—something about how this was happening because she coddled the boy too much. The usual. At least lately.

Kate's stomach clenched, and she dashed up the stairs to her room. Even after she closed the door behind her, she could still hear the muffled shouts through the house's thin walls. She squeezed her eyes shut tight, then glanced at her phone again and slid it into her pocket.

Okay, so maybe it was kind of crazy to even think about spending the night at Fitz's place. But her whole life had gone nuts lately. Besides, wasn't Tommi always telling her to trust people more, to ask for help when she needed it?

She tossed a few things in a duffel bag and headed back downstairs. When she poked her head into the kitchen, her mother was huddled on a stool in front of the old butcher block island. Kate's father was glaring at her from over by the pantry.

"Hey, guys," Kate said. "Um, Nat just called and invited me to sleep over for the weekend. Okay?"

Her father shot her a look, though Kate had a funny feeling he didn't really see her. "Hmm? Oh, fine. Have fun, Katie."

"Okay, thanks." Kate waited a second to see if her mother

would turn to look at her, but she didn't move. "Um, bye," Kate added.

She hurried outside and tossed her bag in the passenger seat. Her hand shook as she turned the key in the ignition, and nerves sparked butterflies in her gut. But she did her best to ignore it. What choice did she have?

NINE

— — — — —

"Urp!" Court patted her stomach. "That was delish."

"See?" Cousin Jon grinned at her. "We do have real restaurants even way down here in the boondocks of Philly, Miss New York Snob."

Court stuck out her tongue at him. Tommi traded an amused glance with Abby. Court and Jon had struck up quite a little flirtation over the course of the group's leisurely dinner at the White Dog Café. It was totally cute, even if Tommi was pretty sure Parker wouldn't think so.

"So is it frat party time?" Mariah asked.

Rashad checked his watch. "It's barely nine," he said. "I doubt those guys have even gone out to buy the beer yet. How about we give you a tour of campus first?"

"Sounds good," Tommi agreed, smiling up at him. During dinner, she'd discovered that Cousin Jon's housemate had more than good looks going for him. That engineering major was no joke—he was really smart, without being a total geek.

His dad was some kind of big-time military officer and he'd lived all over the world, from Amsterdam to Hong Kong. He'd even learned to ride during a stint in Portugal, though his real love was sailing.

They all wandered along Locust Walk, the main pedestrian drag through campus. The guys pointed out various landmarks—the library, a big statue of Ben Franklin, various historic buildings—though Tommi didn't pay much attention to the details. She was just enjoying the warm night air and the relaxed but buzzy vibe. It was pretty obvious that the semester hadn't started yet, but there were still plenty of people around. Some were camped out on the grass, others were just wandering around like Tommi and her friends. It was way different from New York, but still cool.

As they were checking out a bulletin board with a bunch of campus events and stuff pinned to it, Tommi's phone buzzed. She fished it out of her purse. It was a text from Alex:

hope you're having a good time! text me when u get back and maybe we can get together.

"Who's that?" Court leaned closer with an impish smile, shooting a quick look at Rashad to make sure he wasn't close enough to hear. "Maybe your *other* boyfriend checking up on you?"

"Shut up." Tommi tucked the phone away without responding to the text. She was surprised Court had even noticed her little flirtation with Rashad, given her much more extreme and obvious one with Cousin Jon. "It's nothing."

"Yeah, right." Court smirked, then hurried forward to grab Jon by the arm and giggle at whatever he was saying. Tommi smiled and shook her head. The girl was shameless.

Then Rashad turned and crooked a finger at her. "Hey, keep up, Tommi," he said. "We don't want to lose you."

"Coming." She hurried to catch up as the others straggled off down the Walk, trying not to think about Alex. This weekend, tonight, didn't have anything to do with him. She and Rashad were just hanging out. Being friendly. No biggie.

By the time they reached the other end of campus, it was a little after ten. "Guess we might as well head over," Jon said, checking the time. "Long as you girls don't mind being unfashionably early, anyway."

"What the hell, we have no pride." Abby grinned. "Right, ladies?"

"Speak for yourself," Mariah retorted. "But yeah, let's get this party started already. I feel a need to meet some hot college guys, stat."

Loud dance music was pouring out the windows of the fraternity house, but when Tommi and the others entered, there were just a few guys standing around talking and chugging something out of plastic cups. One of the guys glanced up.

"Fresh meat!" he exclaimed with a grin.

Another guy hurried forward. "Welcome, ladies," he said with a goofy little bow. "Come on in and make yourselves at home. Drinks are in there."

He pointed into the next room. All the furniture had been pushed back against the walls, and the music was throbbing out of a large set of speakers perched on the windowsills.

"What are we waiting for?" Mariah said. She led the way into the room, shimmying her hips to the music. Tommi noticed several of the guys hanging out in there watching her.

Abby saw them, too. "Looks like Mariah won't have any trouble meeting hot frat guys," she commented to Tommi.

Tommi grinned. "Yeah."

Before she could say anything else, she felt a tap on her shoulder. Turning, she saw a guy grinning at her. He was tall and clean-cut, with adorable brown curls and nice arms.

"Hi, I'm Chuck," he said. "Wanna dance?"

Tommi hesitated, feeling another brief flash of guilt at the thought of Alex back in New York. But again, she shook it off. The guy was asking her to dance, not to go to the prom or something.

"Sure," she said. "I'm Tommi. Let's dance."

The after-party was a swanky affair with tons of celebrities, a live jazz band, and the longest buffet table Zara had ever seen. She glanced around, sizing up the male members of the crowd. She ignored the stars of the film and most of the other well-known actors, directors, and other Hollywood types. *Way* too old. Plus most of them were friends with her parents.

But there were plenty of hot guys there within an acceptable age range, too. Minor celebs. A sports star or two. Whatever you called the male version of socialite kids.

But she skimmed over all of them, looking for Mr. Leather Jacket. Had he come to the after-party?

She started circulating, nodding to people she knew but being careful to avoid getting pulled in to small talk. The room was growing more crowded all the time; she couldn't even see

Gina anymore, and she was usually hard to miss. It was going to be tough to find one guy in all this . . .

Then she saw a familiar shaggy dark head over by the buffet table. She smiled, quickly adjusting the neckline of her dress and wetting her lips before striding over.

"Hey," she said.

He turned toward her. The leather jacket was gone, revealing broad, somewhat beefy shoulders encased in a silky button-down shirt.

"Oh," he said, a slow smile forming. "Hey. What's up?"

Zara poked one finger into his chest. It hit immediate resistance, indicating some serious muscles under that shirt. Nice.

"First things first," she said, not looking away from him as a waitress slid an empty plate into her hand. "What's your name?"

He chuckled. "Marcus. Sorry, didn't realize I didn't tell you before."

"S'all right." Zara glanced down at the table and snagged a smoked salmon canapé, popping it into her mouth and then adding a couple more to her plate. "So what's your deal, Marcus?"

"My deal? As in, my life story?" He shrugged. "It's boring. But in a nutshell, I'm pretty new to New York. Moved up here after I graduated. Grew up in Texas."

"Wait, you graduated from college already?" Zara said. "I thought you said you're only twenty."

"I am. Guess I must be a genius, huh?" He leaned past her to help himself to some olives. She was tempted to reach up and squeeze the bicep in front of her face, but resisted. For now.

"So where'd you go to college, genius boy?" she asked.

Marcus glanced at her, eyes flashing with amusement. "What is this, an inquisition? Enough about me; I want to hear about you. What's *your* deal?"

"Doesn't the whole world already know?" Zara replied lightly, licking a flake of pastry off her fingers. If he was sucking up to her to get close to her mother, might as well find out up front. Been there, done that.

"Huh?"

Zara shot him a look. His expression was curious but a little confused. She shrugged.

"Sorry, most people already know way too much about me when they ask that question," she said. "Comes with the territory when your parents are famous."

"Who are your parents?"

Was he serious? Zara sized him up, trying to guess his angle. How could he be at an event like this and not recognize her?

"Gina Girard," she said after a moment, deciding to play along. "Zac Trask."

"Oh!" His expression cleared. "Okay, got it. I thought your mom looked familiar earlier. So that's your parents out of the way. What about you?"

She hesitated again. She liked to think she was pretty good at telling when someone was bullshitting her. And she didn't think he was. That was kind of . . . well, different, at least. Intriguing, even.

"Um, I like to have fun," she said, grabbing a couple of deviled eggs with caviar. "But my main thing is horseback riding. I've got a couple of horses I keep at this barn up in Westchester, and I show them a lot."

"Really? Awesome." He took one of the deviled eggs, too. "I rode some down in Texas. Not that much—I'm no expert or anything. But a buddy of mine has a ranch, and well . . . So do you have a boyfriend?"

Zara hid her smile. Okay, so she wasn't the only one who was intrigued. Suddenly she was very glad she'd come tonight, boring movie and all.

"No one special." She picked up her loaded plate and nodded toward some little tables set up in a corner of the room. "Let's go sit down, and I'll tell you whatever else you want to know."

TEN

— — — — —

"So here it is." Fitz finished fiddling with the last of the locks and opened the apartment door with a flourish. "Home sweet home."

Kate stepped inside, so nervous she was afraid she might explode all over the elegant foyer's parquet floor and tastefully muted walls. This was all happening so fast. Fitz had kept her distracted on the drive down here, telling funny stories and being his usual charming self. It had almost felt like any other evening, as if the two of them were just going out to dinner or something. At least until he'd led her up through his luxury building's hushed, carpeted lobby. The higher the elevator had risen, the harder it had been for Kate to breathe. And it wasn't the altitude, even though the apartment *was* on the twenty-third floor.

Fitz grabbed her duffel and followed her inside, letting the door fall shut behind him with a heavy *thunk*. He hit a switch, turning on a row of recessed overhead lights that lit their way down a long, narrow hall lined with framed paintings.

"Come on, I'll give you the grand tour," he said, taking her hand in his. "Living room's this way."

He led her down the hallway and into an enormous room decorated in shades of coffee and beige. Two of the walls were mostly windows, one set offering a spectacular view down Fifth Avenue and the other opening onto a large balcony overlooking Central Park.

"Wow, this place is . . . really nice." The words felt inadequate and kind of stupid, but Kate wasn't sure what else to say. Yes, she'd known that Fitz's family was rich. More money than God—that was how most people put it. It was obvious in everything she already knew about him. His clothes. His string of fancy horses. The casual way he pulled out a credit card to pay for lunch at the diner. Even how he'd jumped in to take the blame for Ford, knowing his parents would make it right.

Kate already knew all that. She did. But right now, standing here in this elegant, expensive room overlooking half of Manhattan, the gulf between them had never felt so vast. Like the two of them didn't even come from the same planet.

He gave a tug on her hand. "Dining room's over here."

She followed him through the formal dining room and the adjacent kitchen, all marble and stainless steel. A quick peek into a luxurious bathroom complete with spa tub and bidet.

"Bedrooms are back this way." Fitz took her through a butler's pantry, past a cozy wood-paneled den, and into another hallway, where he stopped and pushed open the first door. "Here's my room."

Kate's heart started pounding. She stared at Fitz's bed, suddenly very aware that the two of them were here alone, late at night. That he was about to lead her into his bedroom, maybe expecting to lay her down on that bed and . . .

She let out a little gasp. "Oh, I—um, that is, we, urgh . . ."

He glanced down at her, then smiled and squeezed her hand. "And your room's this way," he said, pulling her along to the next doorway. He swung it open, revealing a slightly smaller but tidy and attractive bedroom. "Good thing Mom likes to keep the guest room ready at all times." He shrugged and grinned. "Because honestly? I suck at making up a bed. The sheets always come out all crooked."

Kate smiled, relief flooding through her as he dropped her hand and stepped forward to toss her bag onto the guest bed. "Th-thanks," she said. "I mean, this is nice. Really nice."

"It's yours as long as you need it." He came over and took both of her hands in his. "My folks won't be back until September, and if I bribe the maid they'll never even know you were here." He smiled that crooked little smile of his. "And you know I'd love having you around. All Kate all the time? Heaven."

"Thanks," she said again, that awkward feeling creeping back again. He was being awfully sweet. But she couldn't help wondering—why? What was in this for him? He could easily get a zillion other girls. Girls twice as pretty as her, girls just as wealthy as him. Girls who didn't have to work all day and end up smelling like dirt and hay and horses. Girls who weren't so uptight about everything, who were willing to do more than kiss, who wouldn't make him wait . . .

"You hungry?" Fitz dropped her hands and headed for the hall. "Go ahead and get settled in if you want. I'll rustle us up some snacks, and then maybe we can find something decent on on-demand."

A few minutes later they were ensconced on a squeaky leather sofa in the den. The fabric felt so rich and supple that Kate was almost afraid to touch it. But Fitz had pulled her down beside him and started tossing chips in the general direction of his mouth, clearly unperturbed when crumbs fell all over the sofa and the Oriental rug on the floor.

"What do you feel like watching?" he asked, scanning through the on-screen movie guide. "Comedy, action?"

"Whatever. You choose." Kate tucked her bare feet up under herself, trying to relax.

Fitz chose a movie and hit start, then dropped the remote on the massive wood-block coffee table, grabbed another handful of chips, and leaned back beside Kate. "So did anything interesting happen after I left the barn today?" he asked as the opening credits started to roll. "Our boy do okay in his new turnout?"

Kate couldn't help smiling as she thought about Flame. "Yeah," she said. "He ran around a little at first, but when he realized there was more grass in there, he settled right in and started eating."

"Cool." Fitz crunched down on the chips, chewing with his mouth half open. "You know, I kind of bought him on a whim—"

"You? Doing something impulsive?" Kate feigned shock. "I can't believe that!"

He threw an arm around her shoulders and gave her a squeeze, laughing. "Stop," he said. "I'm being serious. And I was just going to compliment you again on your amazing eye.

Because even I can see now that Flame's going to be awesome once he hits the show ring."

"He is pretty awesome, isn't he?" Kate shivered and smiled as she remembered that day's ride. "I mean, obviously we won't know anything for sure until we try him over some jumps. But the way he takes everything in stride, I'm thinking we can at least set up a cross-rail next time, and then maybe . . ."

The conversation flowed naturally from there; they chatted about Flame's training, other horses at the barn, the upcoming Washington Crossing show, even Summer's Sweet Sixteen party. Then they stopped talking and watched the movie for a while. It was kind of dull, though, and Kate's mind started wandering. Having Flame in the barn was amazing. But at what cost? What if Nat never talked to her again? Kate wasn't sure she could stand that. But she couldn't figure out what to do to fix things, either. This wasn't like the other times she and Nat had fought; Nat wasn't just going to forget she was mad at Kate this time.

Suddenly she realized that Fitz was running his hand up and down her arm. When she glanced over at him, he was staring at her.

"Hey," he said, his voice husky and low.

"Hey," she said quietly, her heart beating faster again.

He pulled her toward him and they kissed, softly at first. But it wasn't long before things got more intense; Kate somehow found herself on his lap, her hands buried in his reddish-blond hair, his hands sliding under her shirt.

Wait, Kate said inside her head. *This isn't—we shouldn't—*

But her brain felt sluggish, and her body didn't really want to stop. Then Fitz suddenly pulled back, sucking in a long breath.

"Sorry," he blurted out. "Um, I mean, it's getting kind of late. We should probably both get some sleep or we'll be dead at the barn tomorrow morning." He shot her a lopsided grin. "I assume you'll want to get there a little earlier than when I normally roll in, at like noon."

"Oh. Right." Kate quickly tugged her shirt back into place, then climbed to her feet. "I mean, yeah, that's a good idea. I mean, um, good night."

"Good night." He stood too, then leaned down and brushed her lips with his once more, soft as a horse's velvety muzzle. "Sleep tight, sweet Kate."

He clicked off the TV, then led the way down the hall to the bedrooms, pausing at his own doorway and watching until she'd reached hers. With one last smile, he disappeared inside.

Kate stood there for a moment, a wave of gratitude almost overwhelming her. What had she been so worried about? Fitz had told her they could take things at her pace, and it was pretty obvious that he meant it.

She let herself into the guest room and fell onto the bed, staring up at the ceiling, which was lit only by the glow of the city outside the windows. Maybe it hadn't been crazy to come here. Maybe this would work out just fine after all.

"Are you kidding me?" Tommi exclaimed. "Truth isn't subjective—it's just, you know, the truth!"

The guy she was talking to leaned closer and grinned. "No

way," he said, tossing his head to get his over-long brown hair out of his eyes. "You should read some Kierkegaard sometime. Truth, like, totally depends on the person who's experiencing it. Or something."

"You're nuts." Tommi waved her beer for emphasis. A little sloshed over the edge of the plastic cup. Oops. But she figured it didn't matter. The couch she was sitting on was even more disgusting than the one in Cousin Jon's house. She took another drink.

Meanwhile the brown-haired guy—Tommi was pretty sure his name was Mike, or possibly Mark—poked her in the shoulder. "Seriously, you really need to educate yourself, dude," he declared. "Because a girl as hot as you shouldn't be so deluded about the basics of, you know, existential thought and stuff."

"Shut up and get me another beer, you pretentious Ivy League asshole." Tommi grinned as the guy laughed, saluted, then hurried off toward the keg in the corner. Okay, she was a little drunk. Maybe even more than a little. But she was having a blast.

The party was in full swing. The later it got, the more people turned up and crowded into the frat house. If the place was this packed now, Tommi couldn't imagine how they'd cram everybody in during the school year.

She glanced around for her friends. Brooke was over by the doorway, flirting with a couple of guys. Court and Jon were dancing in front of one of the speakers. The others were nowhere to be seen.

Leaning back against the couch, Tommi closed her eyes for a second and hummed along with the hip-hop song that was playing. Despite all her earlier angst, she was glad she'd come on this trip. It was good to get away from her normal life once in a while, and this was about as far away as you could get. She'd almost forgotten how people outside of New York weren't nearly as likely to recognize her last name or know much about her or her father. It was kind of cool to feel so anonymous. So free of other people's expectations.

Mike-Mark came back with two overflowing cups. "Here you go, babe." He handed one to her, then sucked the foam off the top of the other. "So anyway, where were we? Oh yeah, Kierkegaard . . ."

They were still arguing about philosophy or something close to it a few minutes later when Rashad appeared. "Yo, Tommi!" His voice was a little louder than normal; his brown eyes a little brighter. "S'up?"

"Dude." Tommi struggled to sit up, spilling more beer onto herself in the process. The couch might be a homemade penicillin experiment, but damn, it was comfy. "Where you been?"

"Looking for you." He grinned and held out his hand. "May I have this dance?"

Tommi stuck out her hand and let him drag her to her feet. "Hey, I was just going to ask her to dance," Mike-Mark complained, his words slurring a little.

"You snooze, you lose, bro." Rashad grinned at him, then half led, half dragged Tommi over to where people were dancing.

Just as they got there, the song changed. "Oh, man!" Tommi rolled her eyes. "Not this one again! This song's *everywhere* these days."

It was "Forgive Me," of course. Rashad started humming along as he pulled her toward him. "Good tune," he commented.

Tommi slid her arms up around his shoulders. "Forgive Me" wasn't really a slow song, but hey, if he wanted to slow dance, that was fine with her. Her arms and legs felt kind of heavy and tired right now anyway.

Soon the two of them were swaying to their own beat. Rashad smelled good—a combination of aftershave, beer, and just a whiff of boy-sweat. Before she realized it, Tommi was burying her nose in his neck and giving a good sniff.

He seemed to like that, at least judging by the way his hands almost immediately slid down to cup her ass. Tommi giggled as he squeezed a bit, then tilted her face up toward him. Before she quite realized what was happening, his mouth locked onto hers, and they were making out. He was a good kisser, though Tommi felt a tiny twinge of guilt for a second.

She couldn't quite remember why, though. And it seemed like way too much effort to figure it out. So she just closed her eyes and let herself enjoy the moment.

ELEVEN

Zara jerked awake as an angry buzz exploded in her left ear. "Shit," she mumbled, grappling under her pillow for the alarm.

She shut it off and let her eyes drift shut again. Then she remembered why the alarm was under there. Muffled, so only she would hear it.

Sitting up, she rubbed her eyes and squinted at the windows. She hated getting up so freaking early. And this time it wasn't even for anything fun, like a horse show.

She stood, groaned, and stretched, then grabbed her watch off her dresser. Six a.m. Ugh.

Padding over to the door, she peeked out into the hall. Her mother's door was closed. No surprise there. They hadn't gotten in until after three last night. Or this morning, technically. In any case, Gina would probably sleep until ten at least.

Still, Zara wasn't taking any chances. She tiptoed down the hall into the guest room and grabbed the pillows and wig out from beneath the sheet, stuffing them back under the bed. She still could hardly believe that lame little trick had worked. Gina had peeked in there last night, whispering a cheery, tipsy "'Night, Stacie!" in the general direction of the lump in the bed.

Next Zara went into the guest bathroom and smeared a little toothpaste around in the sink. She kicked the bath mat askew and wet down one of the towels, leaving it draped over the shower rod.

"You know, I'm damn good at this," she whispered, grinning sleepily at herself in the mirror. "I should probably be, like, a spy or something."

She knew her mother probably wouldn't even look in the guest bathroom. But you never could tell. The more convincing she made things, the easier it would be to skate through these next two days. She could only hope that Gina stuck to her plan to spend the afternoon and evening with some friends who lived way uptown. That would make one full day without Zara having to figure out what else "Stacie" could get up to, which would just leave tomorrow . . .

Zara sighed, rubbing her eyes to chase away the last of the sleep. Sneaking around like this was turning out to be a serious hassle. Definitely more trouble than her usual method of just doing whatever the hell she wanted and screw the consequences. For a second she wondered why she was bothering. It wasn't as if she cared if Stacie got in trouble. Frankly, the girl deserved it.

But that wasn't the point, and she knew it. If she didn't pull this off, she could forget about having any fun for the rest of the summer. Gina would have some uptight Maria von Trapp type here before Zara could say "Hell no."

I can do this, she told herself firmly, glaring at her reflection with renewed purpose. *Gina's easy to distract. Plus she's got a million things going on this weekend as usual. I can totally do this.*

Realizing that time was passing while she stood there giving herself a rah-rah pep talk, Zara headed back to her own room. She pulled on her riding clothes without bothering to shower. What was the point? She was just going to end up smelling like horse anyway. Besides, the car service she'd called yesterday was probably already waiting downstairs. The last thing she wanted was for the driver to get impatient and buzz her from the lobby. Gina was a light sleeper.

She tiptoed downstairs to the message center. Grabbing one of the notepads from the basket, she quickly scribbled a note:

Mom,

Stacie and I had to leave before you woke up—she's driving me to the barn. We'll grab some lunch up there and be back tonight.

See you,

Z

Soon she was slipping out the door, boots in hand. Yeah, she could do this. In forty-eight hours her mother would be on a plane back to Vancouver, and everything would go back to normal. Or at least as normal as Zara's life ever got.

Kate drifted awake out of a confusing dream about Nat yelling at Jamie. She cracked one eye open and glanced to her left to see how long she had until the alarm went off. But instead of her familiar bedside table and blinking alarm clock, she saw nothing but a wall covered in pale green-and-cream-striped wallpaper. Huh?

She gasped and sat bolt upright in a panic. Only then did her brain catch up to her eyes. Oh, right. She was in Fitz's guest room. She just sat there for a moment, feeling strange, as if she might still be dreaming. Could she really be *living* with her boyfriend right now?

Then she noticed the clock on the cherrywood dresser. It was almost six thirty. "Oh, no!" she gasped aloud. She usually tried to get to the barn by seven on Saturdays.

Grabbing her jeans off the cute little slipper chair where she'd dropped them last night, she yanked them on, then scrabbled in her duffel for a clean T-shirt. She ducked into the en suite bathroom just long enough to splash water on her face, pull her hair into a sloppy ponytail, and brush her teeth. Then she hurried for the door, wondering how long it would take her to drag Fitz out of bed.

The scents of fresh coffee and pancakes greeted her as she stepped into the hallway. Following her nose to the kitchen, she found Fitz standing at the stove, dressed in pajama pants and an oversized Knicks T-shirt. He was using a spatula to poke at several sizzling round blobs cooking on a large griddle pan.

He glanced up when he heard her enter. "Morning, sunshine," he said with a grin. "I remembered you like pancakes."

"Huh?" Kate blinked at him, her mind already halfway to Pelham Lane.

"Pancakes." He waved his spatula for emphasis, dribbling

batter onto the floor. "You ordered them at the diner the other day, right?"

"Oh! Yeah, I love pancakes." Kate sneaked a peek at her watch. "I'm not sure I have time to eat them right now, though. It's a long drive up to the barn, and I'm supposed to—"

"Chill, I took care of it," Fitz cut her off. "You left your phone in the den last night, so I used it to text Jamie that you're running late today. He said no problem, come in whenever." He shrugged. "Hope you don't mind. I thought maybe you wouldn't want everyone to know your business, so I pretended the texts were from you. You know."

"Yeah. Thanks." Kate was touched and a little surprised that he'd thought of that. He wasn't exactly the shy type, but he must have guessed that she wouldn't be comfortable having people know that she was staying with him. Even Jamie. "Are you sure he's not mad?"

"Are you kidding? He actually said, and I quote, 'Take your time.' And if Jamie says that, you know he means it." Fitz slid the spatula under one of the browning pancakes and flipped it. It landed half over the edge of the griddle, but he grabbed it with his fingers and tossed it onto a plate sitting on the counter nearby. "Breakfast will be served in just a minute," he told Kate. "Go sit down—I poured you some juice. There's coffee too if you want it."

"Thanks," Kate said again, feeling herself relax at least a little. "Need any help?"

"Nope. Sit." He pointed to the large marble-topped kitchen island, then turned to flip another pancake onto the plate.

Kate wandered over to the island and slid onto one of the

stools set along the far side. Fitz had already set two places there, complete with cloth napkins, glasses of water and orange juice, and even a little vase with a flower in it. Taking a sip of her OJ, she leaned her chin on her hand, watching him cook.

Okay, it still felt kind of weird to be here. But she was starting to think that maybe she could get used to this.

"I'm never drinking again," Abby moaned, hunching over her steaming cup of coffee.

Tommi took a bite of her bagel. She and her girlfriends were slumped at a table in a coffeeshop just off campus. "I know, right?" she said. "I lost count of how many beers I had."

"Beers?" Court grinned, looking way too chipper for the amount of sleep they'd all had. "*I* lost count of how many cute college guys were drooling all over you, Tommi. Including the mega yummy Rashad, of course. I was half expecting to find you in his room this morning."

"I'm surprised you could see what Tommi was doing while you were slobbering all over my cousin," Brooke retorted with a smirk.

Tommi didn't say anything, just smiled down into her latte. Yeah, she'd felt better. But a minor hangover was a small price to pay for last night. It had been a long time since she'd cut loose and just had fun like that. Way too long.

"Our Tommi was definitely the belle of the ball." Abby stirred the fourth packet of sugar into her cappuccino. "Good thing Alex wasn't around to see it."

"Yeah, well." Tommi shrugged, feeling a little uncomfortable. And this time the hangover had nothing to do with it. "So what are we going to do today, girls?"

Her friends traded an amused glance. "Okay, guess we're changing the subject," Mariah said. "Fair enough. Once we've got enough caffeine in us to feel semi-human again, what about hitting up the university bookstore? I promised my dad I'd bring him back a Penn T-shirt."

As her friends started chatting about the day's plans, Tommi remembered that she hadn't checked her messages yet that morning. Or last night, either. She'd been too busy to think about it.

Pulling out her phone, she glanced at it. Two voice mails, both left fairly late last night, and half a dozen texts.

She scrolled through the texts first, stopping when she got to one from Alex. Short and sweet, just a cute little note saying he'd thought of her when he heard a certain song, yadda yadda.

Tommi bit her lip. They'd never talked about being exclusive or anything. Still, she had a feeling he'd be hurt if he knew about last night. She couldn't quite dredge up much regret, though. Guilt? Sure, a little. Regret? Not really.

She skipped past the text without responding, scanning the others—just goofy or unimportant messages from various friends. Then she moved on to the voice mails. The first, to her surprise, was from Grant.

She just stared at his name on the screen for a second. Sure, they were friends. But not the type who talked all that much. She hadn't heard from him since he'd started dating Zara a few weeks back. Why was he calling her now?

Then she shrugged, realizing there was one easy way to find out. She put the phone to her ear to listen.

"Hey, Tommi, it's me, Grant. Sorry to bother you, uh, it's just . . ."

His voice sort of trailed off for a second, mumbling incoherently. Tommi pressed the phone closer to her ear. He sounded weird. Drunk, maybe?

". . . and uh, so the thing is, Zara just dumped me. At least I think she did. Mumble-mumble this weird text about seeing other people, or, uh. So anyway, got any idea what's up with her? I tried to text her back but she didn't answer."

There was a loud sniffle. Then a pause, long enough that Tommi thought he was finished.

"Anyway," he went on. *"Uh, thanks. You know, if you can help. Bye."*

Tommi lowered the phone and stared at it, letting out a sigh. Abby glanced over.

"What's wrong?" she asked, her voice muffled by a mouthful of cinnamon bagel. "You going to call Alex and tell him you're leaving him for a hot college man?"

Tommi rolled her eyes. "Just checking my messages," she said, trying to sound casual.

But the truth was, she was feeling tense. She definitely hadn't wanted to get in the middle of this whole Grant-Zara thing.

She scrolled to the next voice mail. It was from someone named Adam Dane. That sounded vaguely familiar, though it took her a second to place it. Oh, right. Adam Dane was a hotshot young trainer who'd just moved to the New York area.

His new facility was only a few miles from Pelham Lane, though Tommi didn't really know him—she'd mostly just seen him at the shows.

"Hey, Tommi, this is Adam Dane," the message began. "Ran into Jamie tonight at a dinner party. He was telling me about the jumper horse you've got for sale, and it sounds interesting. I was hoping I could bring a client of mine to see it tomorrow. Text me and let me know what time works for you."

Tommi groaned, lowering the phone. Wasn't she supposed to be on vacation? She so didn't feel like dealing with business right now.

This time Brooke was the one who looked over. "What?" she asked.

"Just this guy wanting to look at Legs," Tommi said. When her friends all stared at her, looking confused, Tommi smiled. "Legs is the name of the horse I'm selling," she clarified. "This local trainer wants to come try him out today. Only duh, I'm not there."

Court shrugged. "So blow it off."

That was tempting. But Tommi knew she couldn't do it. Not if she wanted her father to take her seriously with this whole horse-training deal. Not if she wanted to take *herself* seriously.

"No biggie. I'll just text him back," she told her friends, her thumbs already flying over the keyboard as she composed a quick response, explaining that she was out of town but would be happy to set up an appointment when she got back to New York.

TWELVE

— — — — —

"Hi, Zara! I was hoping you'd come out today."

Zara winced. Summer. Of freaking course. She should have known a relaxing day at the barn was out of the question.

"Yeah, I'm here." Zara kept walking, heading for the tack room. "Call the press."

Summer trotted along behind her. "So you'll never guess what I decided to get for my party," she said. "A fortune-teller!" she added without so much as a two-second pause to actually let Zara guess. Not that Zara had intended to do so. "Won't that be a blast?"

"I suppose. See you around, okay? Gotta get my riding stuff." Zara ducked into the tack room, hoping Summer would take the hint.

No such luck.

"Anyway," Summer said, stopping in the doorway, "I also talked my mom into letting me hire these shiatsu masseuses she uses sometimes for the party. They're twins, and they just moved here from Japan like five years ago, but they treat all the important people in New York. There will be a little room set up near the ballroom with tables and aromatherapy and Japanese music and stuff, just like a real spa, and guests can just drop in for a free massage anytime they want. It'll be amazing, don't you think?"

"Stunning. Here, hold this." Zara shoved her Antares at Summer. Summer looked startled. Then she glanced down at the saddle and smiled.

"This is a really nice saddle," she said. "I was thinking about getting one just like it. If Mom and Daddy get me another hunter for my birthday, I might think about getting a custom saddle made for it."

"Hmm." Zara grabbed her bridle and grooming kit and headed out of the tack room. She didn't bother to check whether Summer followed. She knew she would.

She headed for the nearest grooming stall. Summer was still blathering about her party, but this time Zara didn't even bother pretending to listen. She'd spent most of the car ride up stressing over how to keep her Stacie scam going for that key final day and a half. She hadn't had any brilliant ideas yet, so instead she let her mind drift back to last night. Specifically, Marcus.

Marcus. Sigh. She was pretty sure that little hearts and butterflies fluttered up from her when she even thought about him. That didn't happen too often, and she wasn't sure how long it would last. But for now, she'd take it. At least it kept her mind off the whole stupid Stacie situation.

"Do you have a lesson with Jamie today?" Summer asked

as she set Zara's saddle on the rack in the grooming stall. "He wants me to do a couple before we leave for Washington Crossing. But I'm not sure I'll have time, what with all the party planning. It's crazy! I have so many tastings and stuff I can barely fit them all in."

"No lesson. Just hacking." Zara hung up her bridle—specifically, Keeper's bridle. She'd planned to do a fun, easy ride on him today. Until Summer had mentioned it, she'd almost forgotten that the Washington Crossing show was coming up so soon.

Zara frowned, realizing that the horses would be leaving for the show in just a couple of days. She'd barely ridden Ellie in the past week, and she was sure Jamie had noticed. He noticed *everything* that went on at his barn. Maybe she should change her plans, ask Jamie if she could do a quick schooling session on the mare instead of hacking Keeper? The trainer would probably eat that up.

Her phone buzzed, interrupting her thoughts. Zara smiled when she saw who the text was from.

Last night was fun. Can we get together again sometime? Marcus

Zara smiled. *Major* hearts and butterflies.

"What?" Summer peered at her. "Are you okay? You look weird. Did you get a text from your parents? Are they coming to my party?"

"Nope, sorry," Zara said. "It's just a friend."

Shoving her phone back in the pocket of her breeches, she headed out of the grooming stall. Minutes later she was clipping a lead shank onto Keeper's halter. Okay, so she knew

Jamie would probably love for her to school Ellie instead. But since when did Zara do what anyone else wanted her to do? She just wasn't in the mood for practicing relaxed canter departs and counting strides and stuff like that today.

She led her horse into the grooming stall and clipped him into the cross-ties. Summer was still chirping away about her party, but her soliloquy about the guest list or whatever was interrupted by a breathless call of "Sorry, sorry, I'm here!" from farther down the aisle.

Glancing out of the grooming stall, Zara saw Kate jogging along. She was pink-faced, and her hair was a total wreck. Not that that was anything new. The girl was cute, but she seriously needed a personal stylist.

Summer saw her, too. "Where were you?" she demanded. "I was looking for you earlier to clean up this really gross bird poop on my horse's stall window."

"Sorry, I'm way late today," Kate said. "Have you guys seen Jamie? Did he get tacked up for the first lesson okay?"

Zara didn't bother to listen to Summer's reply. For one thing, she was too surprised. She was pretty sure this had to be the first time ever that she'd arrived at the barn before Kate. She wouldn't have been surprised to find out the girl actually slept in a spare stall.

"So, Little Miss Tardy," she said with a smirk. "Hot date last night or something? We've all been there."

Kate shot her a startled glance, then smiled uncertainly. "Um, no, just, um, you know. Overslept."

"Whatever." Zara could tell from Kate's expression that there was probably more to the story, but she wasn't going to push it. Turning toward Keeper, she clucked for him to lift his hoof so she could pick it out. Time to get him tacked up so she could get away from Summer and go back to thinking about Marcus.

"Good boy." Zara gave Keeper a pat, then swung down from the saddle right outside the barn doors. She'd had a nice ride, starting off in the ring and then going for a short hack around one of the pastures. She was running up her stirrups when Miguel bustled past pushing a wheelbarrow full of shavings.

"Have a good ride?" the head groom asked, pausing. "Need any help untacking?"

"It's okay, I've got it," Zara told him. "Thanks anyway."

Miguel nodded and moved on. Zara led Keeper inside and into one of the wash stalls. Someone had turned on a radio somewhere nearby, and it was playing that crazy catchy "Forgive Me" song that was topping the charts right now. Zara smirked, knowing how her father would grumble if he heard it—he hated that kind of bubblegum pop, though he'd never admit it in public.

She hummed along with the song as she quickly pulled off Keeper's tack and hosed him down. She was in a good mood. Not only had the ride been fun, but she'd spent much of it imagining all the ways she and Marcus might "get together," as he'd texted. It was definitely a nice change of pace from thinking about Stacie all the freaking time.

Soon Keeper was back in his stall, munching on the handful of baby carrots Zara had swiped from the barn fridge. She turned the horse's fan up to high, then gave him a pat. When she turned away, she saw Ellie watching her from the next stall.

"Hey, girlie." Zara stepped over and fished one last carrot out of her pocket. She felt a pang of guilt as the mare crunched down on it. Should she take Ellie out for a quick flatwork session at least? Maybe even see if Jamie could squeeze her in for a lesson today?

Before she could decide, she heard a shout from around the corner. Then a burst of loud laughter.

"Better go see what's going on." Zara gave Ellie one last pat, then hurried down the aisle.

When she rounded the corner, she saw a small crowd gathered outside the tack room. In the center of it was Dani. She was leaning on her crutches, grinning as Marissa, Fitz, and Summer chattered at her excitedly. Oh, and Kate was there, too, right inside the tack room—it took Zara an extra moment to notice her, since she was just standing there with a broom in one hand, smiling at Dani but being quiet as a mouse. As usual.

"Hey," Zara said, hurrying over to join in. "How's it going, Dani?"

"Great, now that I'm here!" Dani hobbled over and threw her arms around Zara, squeezing her into a tight hug. "I've missed all you guys so much! I even missed the smell of horse manure!"

"Are you saying I smell like horse manure?" Zara joked, a little breathless after the girl's super enthusiastic hug.

"Ha!" Dani barked. "No, not you, sorry. Just—just everything! I've been so bored at home!"

Zara smiled. "I hear you." It was cute how excited Dani was to be back.

"Guess what, Zara," Summer said. "Even though Dani obviously can't ride in the show, she's still coming to my party."

"Wouldn't miss it." Dani grinned. "It's, like, the social event of the season, right?"

"Totally!" Summer replied, though Zara caught Fitz rolling his eyes in the background.

"Come in here, you guys," Fitz spoke up, cocking his head toward the tack room. "Marissa and I were just helping Kate knock the cobwebs out of the corners."

Zara drifted into the room along with the others. Fitz and Marissa grabbed the other two brooms, so she just perched on the bandage trunk next to Summer. "So what have you been doing while you can't ride?" she asked Dani, who was carefully lowering herself onto a stool.

Dani sighed. "Being bored to death, mostly," she said. "My parents want me to, like, get started on my school's fall reading list. Can you believe it? I told them I'm not *that* bored."

Marissa laughed. "Seriously!"

"Anyway, I've mostly just been reading magazines and messing around online and stuff." Dani shrugged. "But enough about my boring life—what's been going on with you guys? It's so so great to be at the barn again! I feel almost like our group lesson just finished and we're waiting for the pizza to come . . ."

"Yeah, except that Tommi's not here," Summer pointed out.

Zara realized she was right. "She's probably out schooling one of her horses or something," she said.

"Nope." Marissa shook her head. "She's away this weekend.

Went to help one of her friends from school move into college down in Philadelphia."

"Oh." Zara shrugged. "Sorry, must have missed that. I've been a little, um, distracted lately."

"Do tell!" Dani's eyes lit up, and she leaned closer. "Have anything to do with that cute guy you were seeing? What was his name again—Greg or something?"

Zara wrinkled her nose. "You mean Grant? Nah, he's history." She hesitated, half tempted to tell them about Marcus. But she held back, not wanting to jinx things.

"So why are you so distracted?" Marissa asked Zara.

Zara shrugged again. "My mom's in town for a few days."

"Really?" Summer said before she could go on. "Wait, I thought you said she was out of the country, and that's why she can't come to my party?"

"She is," Zara said. "I mean, she was—and she will be again soon. She flies back to Vancouver on Monday."

"Oh." Summer's face fell. "Well, speaking of my party, Dani, you'll never believe the menu the caterers have planned . . ."

Zara was saved from paying attention to any more of that by the buzz of her phone. She pulled it out and saw that it was a text from Grant. Speak of the devil.

She scanned the message:

I need to talk to u. pls give me 1 more chance?

Zara frowned. The guy didn't give up, did he? She deleted the text, then stuck the phone back in her pocket.

"Hey Dani," she said, interrupting Summer's usual party blather. "Got a pen? We should all totally sign your cast."

Kate finished decobwebbing and set aside her broom. She'd only been half listening to Summer talk about her Sweet Sixteen party. When everyone started clamoring to sign Dani's cast, Kate took advantage of the distraction and slipped toward the door.

"Where you going, gorgeous?" Fitz asked, stepping over and touching her on the shoulder.

She forced a smile. "I'll be back in a bit. Just need to take care of a few other quick chores."

Ducking out before he could respond, she hurried down the aisle without looking back. It was true—she really did have about a million things to do. And no wonder, considering she'd arrived at the barn a full hour and a half later than usual. As sweet as Fitz was being, she couldn't help feeling a flash of annoyance about that. Why had he let her sleep so late, knowing she was supposed to be at work? In any case, while she was glad to see Dani back at the barn, Kate definitely didn't have time to hang out all day.

Besides that, she really needed a few minutes alone. It was weird being with Fitz 24/7. He took up a lot of space in a room, leaving her feeling like she barely had time to breathe, let alone think.

Stepping into an empty stall, she pulled her cell phone out of the back pocket of her jeans and flipped it open. She hesitated for just a second before punching in a familiar number.

"Katie?" Her father's voice sounded weary and a little distracted. "Hey, everything okay?"

"Sure. I was just calling to, um, check in." Kate bit her lip. "You know—find out how everything's going."

"It's going." His clipped tone told her all she needed to know.

"Oh. Well, I was thinking, since I'm leaving for this next show early Tuesday . . ." She took a deep breath. "Uh, Nat wants me to stay for the rest of the weekend and take off straight from her place. Is that all right?"

"Hmm." There was a pause, and Kate was pretty sure she heard the sound of shuffling papers in the background. Was he even paying attention? "Natalie's parents okay with that plan?" he asked.

"Yeah, they're fine with it." Kate hated lying to her father. Actually she hated lying, period. But in this case, it definitely beat the alternative.

Another pause. "Okay," her father said at last. "Might as well get in your fun before school starts, eh? Tell Nat and her folks I said hi."

"I will. Thanks, Dad." Kate clutched the phone to her ear, a sudden wave of something—regret? nostalgia?—washing over her. "See you next Sunday."

She hung up, then stared at her phone for a second. What if her father decided to call Nat's house to check up on her? Normally it wouldn't be an issue. Kate had covered for Nat zillions of times when she wanted to sneak around with a guy or something. Should Kate try calling her, tell her what was going on? It had been almost a week, and Nat had a short attention span. Maybe she'd calmed down about the whole Flame thing by now.

Then again, maybe not. When it came right down to it, Kate didn't quite have the nerve to find out. Not now, with so much else on her mind. She'd just have to take her chances. Anyway, her father trusted her. And with everything else that was going on, he probably wouldn't even remember she was gone.

She stuck the phone in her pocket and stepped out of the stall. Thinking about Nat had reminded her—she hadn't visited Flame yet today. Checking her front pocket for the peppermints she'd stuck in there earlier, she hurried down the aisle.

Tommi leaned on her elbow, texting with one hand.

"What are you doing? Checking in with the boyfriend?" Abby asked lazily, barely flicking her dark brown eyes toward Tommi. All five girls were hanging out on College Green, the grassy open area at the center of campus. The humidity that had been hanging over the entire Eastern Seaboard had lifted, resulting in a perfect late-summer day. Dozens of people were reading, sleeping, or sunbathing on the grass, while others wandered along the pedestrian walkways that crisscrossed the green.

"Not even close," Tommi told Abby. "I'm just texting my friend Kate. You know—seeing how everything's going at the barn."

Court rolled her eyes. She was deathly afraid of the sun, so she was wearing a wide-rimmed straw hat and a gauzy long-sleeved linen shirt.

"You are seriously addicted to that place, Aaronson," she commented, fanning a gnat away from her face. "There's more to life than horses, you know."

Tommi just shrugged, not bothering to explain that she wasn't texting to check in on her horses. She knew Jamie and his staff were on top of that. She just wanted to touch base with Kate, make sure she was okay and remembering to eat. She sent the text, then sat up and stretched.

"So what are we going to do later?" she asked the others.

Brooke glanced up from the course catalog she was flipping through. "I told Jon and Rashad we'd meet up with them before dinner," she said. "Until then, guess we're on our own. Anybody have any brilliant ideas?"

Tommi shook her head, and Court just shrugged.

"I'm happy staying here and working on my tan," Abby said.

Mariah didn't answer. She was watching a guy walk past. He was clean-cut and broad-shouldered, dressed in khaki shorts and a Penn Lacrosse T-shirt.

"Be careful, M," Court told her with a smirk. "You're drooling."

"What?" Mariah swiped at her mouth, then frowned. "Very funny."

Abby laughed. "Hey, I don't blame you. Plenty of eye candy around here." She glanced over at a bookishly handsome guy in his twenties reading on a bench nearby.

Tommi nodded. It was so easy to get caught up in her little worlds of barn-school-friends, so easy to forget there was a whole other world out there. Even living in a city the size of New York.

"I could hang out here all day," she commented, turning to squint at a trio of guys playing Frisbee nearby. "I love people watching."

"Me too. At least when those people are hot college men."
Court grinned.

Tommi didn't answer. One of the Frisbee guys had just turned to retrieve a wild kick and caught her staring. Oops. Tommi almost turned away.

But she shrugged off the impulse. What the hell? This weekend was about trying new things, right? That included meeting new people.

"Nice moves!" she called out, waving to Mr. Frisbee.

He looked surprised. His buddies turned to see what was going on, and almost immediately started ribbing him.

Brooke giggled. "Nice work, Tommi. I think you just made that nerd's day."

"Shut up, he's not a nerd." Tommi watched the guy's cheeks turn red. "Okay, maybe he's a *little* nerdy, but that's cool. I like smart guys."

Moments later, Mr. Nerd and his two friends were standing over the girls. "Hi there, ladies," one of the other guys said. "How's it going? Gabe here wanted to come over and say hello."

He shoved Mr. Nerd—aka Gabe—toward Tommi. Gabe stumbled over Court's Diet Coke can, spilling it onto the grass, then shot all the girls a sheepish grin.

"Uh, yeah," he said. "That is, I was just about to head over to the University Museum for this lecture, right? It's about ancient Egypt. I thought maybe some of you might want to go. It should be really interesting—I had the prof who's giving the talk for Anthro last semester, and he's a really good speaker."

"So you're upperclassmen?" Abby sat up, suddenly looking more interested.

"Sophomores," Gabe said. "This is Jared, and that's Keith."

"Are you an anthropology major?" Tommi asked Gabe. "I always thought that kind of stuff sounded really interesting."

"You did?" Mariah asked. "Funny you never mentioned it before."

Tommi ignored her, smiling at Gabe. "Anyway, I'd love to check out that lecture. When's it start?"

THIRTEEN

— — — · — —

Zara yawned as she wandered into the barn office the next morning. There was a coffeemaker in there, and she was in serious need of caffeine. Jamie was sitting behind the desk, bent over some paperwork.

"Hey," Zara greeted him.

Jamie glanced up. "Oh! Zara." His surprise was obvious. "You're here early."

No kidding. Zara had left the loft at the crack of dawn again. Hey, it had worked yesterday, right? Gina had been long gone for her friends' place by the time Zara had arrived back in the city, and Zara had made sure she and "Stacie" were both in bed by the time her mother got home late that night.

"Well, I'm glad you're taking your riding so seriously." Jamie leaned back in his chair, studying her. "I'm sure the results will show at Washington Crossing. How's Ellie feeling to you these days?"

"I'll let you know in a while." Zara crossed to the coffeepot and grabbed one of the paper cups stacked beside it. "Is it okay if I hack her this morning?"

"Sure," Jamie said, looking pleased. "I think that would be good for both of you."

"Cool." Zara had come to the barn without any particular plan in mind, aside from getting "Stacie" away from Gina. But what the hell, she was here now. Might as well ride, right? And if doing so happened to get her on Jamie's good side at the same time? Bonus.

She poured herself half a cup of coffee and gulped it down on the way to Ellie's stall. It looked as if the grooms had just brought her in from the overnight turnout field. There was a fresh pile of hay in her stall, and nobody had brushed the dirt out of her mane yet.

"Come on, girlie—it's you and me today," she said, scratching the mare in her favorite spot under the jaw. Ellie snorted and nosed at her hopefully, and Zara smiled and dug into her pocket, coming up with a slightly dusty breath mint. The horse slurped it up as Zara slipped on her halter.

Zara was leading the mare out of her stall when her phone rang. Uh-oh—it was Gina.

"Hi, Mom," she said, tucking the phone between shoulder and face as she clipped Ellie into the cross-ties. "What's up? Sorry we missed you this morning."

"Me too, love," Gina said. "Especially since I probably won't be here when you get home later."

Zara's heart jumped. "Really?" she asked, carefully keeping the sudden surge of excitement out of her voice. She couldn't seriously get this lucky, could she? "How come?"

"Do you remember Hal and Crystal? She played my sister in that thriller I did a couple of years back, and he—"

"Yeah, I remember them," Zara broke in. "Why?"

"They've got a place out in the Hamptons, and when they heard I was in town, they insisted I come out and stay. Wouldn't take no for an answer." Her musical laugh chimed in Zara's ear. "But I promise to come home early enough tomorrow to spend some quality time with you and Stacie before my flight, okay?"

"Sure, no problem." Zara felt like jumping up and down, but she kept her cool. "We'll see you in the morning."

She hung up, then let out a whoop. Ellie leaped in place, pulling back at the cross-ties with her head up and her eyes rolling.

"Oops. Sorry, girlie. It's okay, babycakes." Zara continued talking and clucking to the horse until she calmed down. Even after Ellie was relaxed again—well, as relaxed as she ever got, anyway—Zara just stood there stroking the mare's neck, deep in thought. "Okay, so I'm off the hook for tonight," she said, more to herself than the mare. "What about tomorrow morning?"

She had no idea. Then she shrugged. Why stress about it right now? She'd come this far. She could figure out a way to get through one more day.

When Zara led Ellie back to her stall an hour and a half later, she found Summer lurking in the aisle nearby. "Oh, good, you're here," Summer exclaimed, hurrying over. She had her breeches rolled up to the knees and flip-flops flapping on her feet.

Wish I could say the same to you, Zara thought. But she wasn't in quite a bitchy enough mood to say it. Ellie had been a little difficult today, balking at Zara's leg every time they passed the gate and blowing at least half her lead changes. But whatever. They'd gotten through it. Besides, Zara was still riding the high from her mother's phone call earlier.

"Hi," she said instead. She gestured toward the Burberry tote lying near the stall door. "You'd better move your bag before Ellie steps on it."

Summer grabbed the bag and moved aside to let the mare pass. "You'll never believe this." Summer's pale blue eyes were wide, and she was grinning like a loon—basically she looked even more psychotic than usual.

"Yeah, you're probably right," Zara said, leading Ellie into her stall and unclipping her halter.

"Huh?" Summer blinked, looking confused. Then she shook her head. "No, seriously, listen—my Sweet Sixteen just got mentioned on HorseShowSecrets!"

Zara came out of the stall. "Horse show what?"

"HorseShowSecrets!" Summer repeated. "You know, that hot new blog?"

"What the hell are you talking about?" Zara hung Ellie's halter on its hook outside the stall, then peeled off her gloves.

"Come on, you must know about it. Here, I'll show you." Summer dug into the tote and pulled out her smartphone. She fiddled with it for a second, then shoved it in Zara's face. "See? It's this brand-new blog—it just started, like, last week or something."

"Oh." Zara gave the tiny screen a cursory glance, then

shrugged. "I don't pay much attention to blogs. I'd rather live my own life than read about someone else's."

"Okay, but this is different." Summer kept waving her phone at Zara. "It talks all about who's winning, who's hooking up, what different trainers are doing, stuff like that from all the biggest A barns and shows. Here's the entry on my party, see?"

A blog all about the A circuit? That piqued Zara's interest enough to grab the phone out of Summer's hand. She scanned the screen.

"Isn't that cool?" Summer was so excited she was practically vibrating. "See the part where it says my party is 'the social event of the season for the junior set'?"

"Yeah, I see it." Zara scrolled down, checking out the next few entries. There was something about a girl who'd fallen off her pricey new imported warmblood at the last show, and a short entry mentioning some rumor about a trainer dating one of his students.

Then her eye caught on the next headline—specifically, her own name. ROCK 'N' ROLL WILD CHILD ZARA TRASK ON HER OWN IN THE BIG CITY.

Zara frowned, scanning the brief article beneath. It wasn't anything too exciting—just a blurb about how both of Zara's famous parents were off being famous elsewhere, leaving their only daughter to brave the big city and the A circuit on her own all summer. Certainly not the worst thing she'd ever read about herself online. Still, it made her feel a little edgy, given the circumstances. What if Gina saw it and started asking tough questions?

Just then Joy hurried by with a feed bucket in each hand. She stopped short when she noticed Summer's outfit.

"Summer," she said briskly, "no sandals in the barn, remember? Get some boots on or get out."

"Oops." Summer shot the assistant trainer a sickly sweet smile and dug into her tote. "They're right in here—I was about to put them on."

Joy nodded and moved on as Summer leaned against the wall and kicked off her flip flops. "Ugh, my feet are soooo sweaty it's disgusting," she complained, wriggling her toes. Her toenails were painted a repulsive shade of glitter pink. Zara was glad when Summer started pulling a pair of boot socks over them. Okay, so the socks were pink, too. Still better.

She glanced down at Summer's phone as it beeped in her hand. "You just got an e-mail," she said, holding out the phone.

"Who's it from?" Summer was yanking on one of her boots by now. "Is it the caterers? They're supposed to let me know if they can get this special kind of cheese that has to be imported from Belgium. You know, to match my horse, since he's a Belgian Warmblood."

Zara rolled her eyes. Her good mood had faded after seeing her name on that blog, and she definitely didn't feel like playing social secretary to Summer, of all people. She was about to say so when she noticed that Joy had stopped just a couple of stalls down to drop off one of her buckets. Zara bit her tongue. She was still technically on probation at Pelham Lane. Telling Summer off just wasn't worth it.

"Uh, it's not from the caterers," she said. "Not unless their e-mail handle is HeatherB."

"It's from Heather?" Summer looked up and smiled. "Cool! That's a friend of mine from the very first barn I ever rode at. Is she coming to the party?"

Zara scanned the e-mail. "Yeah, she says she's really psyched about the party and can't wait to see you again, blah blah. Says she even dug up an old photo of the two of you at a horse show with your ponies." She scrolled down, a little curious to check out what kind of psycho loser would actually be excited to see Summer. When she got a look at the attached picture, her eyes widened. "Whoa!" she exclaimed. "Is that really you?"

Summer's face went pale. "Give me that," she yelped, leaping to her feet with one boot still only half on. She grabbed the phone out of Zara's hand, quickly deleting the e-mail. "You can't tell anyone," she said, her voice shaking. "Please, Zara!"

Kate stared out the car window at the lights of the Triborough Bridge, which looked smeary and unreal through the misty summer rain that had started falling halfway down the Hutchinson River Parkway. She couldn't believe it was already Sunday evening. Glancing at the clock on the dashboard of Fitz's car, she grimaced. Not even 7:00 p.m. If Fitz hadn't gotten impatient and made her leave, she'd still be at the barn helping Miguel and Elliot turn horses out for the night. Or maybe pulling manes or sweeping out the horse trailers or organizing supplements. Or any of the other ten zillion things still left to do before they all packed up to leave for the Washington Crossing show early Tuesday morning.

"So what should we do for dinner?" Fitz asked.

Kate glanced over, distracted by the list of tomorrow's tasks she'd just started in her head. "Dinner?" she echoed blankly.

"Yeah." He shot her a look. "You know, that meal people have at the end of the day?"

Kate forced a smile. "Um, I don't care. Anything you want is fine. I'm not that hungry."

"You sure? Because there's a new Thai place on Seventy-Seventh I've been wanting to try out."

Kate's mind had already started drifting again, but she jerked back to attention. "A restaurant?"

"Yeah. You know, one of those places people go to eat out." Fitz's playful tone had a slight edge to it this time. Or was that Kate's imagination?

"Sorry. I'm just kind of tired." Kate forced a smile. "I was thinking we could eat in tonight."

She tried to keep her voice pleasant. It was pretty obvious that Fitz was getting impatient with her, and she couldn't really blame him. She'd barely heard a word he'd said since leaving the barn. She felt a twinge of guilt. He was doing so much for her and being so sweet, letting her stay with him all weekend.

On the other hand, she couldn't help feeling a little impatient herself. He knew how important her job was to her.

"Fine," he said. "I guess we can order in." He swerved to avoid an SUV that had just drifted into his lane and let out a curse. "Man, I hate driving in the rain. People suck."

They didn't talk much for the rest of the drive. Once they reached the apartment, Kate headed straight for the shower. She stood under the hot water for a long time, grateful not to have Andy pounding on the door, yelling for her to hurry up.

When she finally emerged, clean and warm and feeling a little more human, she noticed the scents of garlic and tomato sauce drifting into the guest room. She pulled on a T-shirt and a pair of sweatpants and padded down to the kitchen in her bare feet.

Fitz was standing in front of the stove, using a wooden spoon to stir something that was sizzling in a large pan. He glanced over when he heard her come in.

"Decided I didn't feel like takeout." He grinned. "Hope you like spaghetti marinara."

"Sure," Kate said. "I mean, yeah, of course. Thanks for cooking—you didn't have to do that."

"I know." He stepped over and kissed her. "I wanted to."

All traces of the earlier snippiness were gone. Fitz was just Fitz again—happy and carefree. "Can I help?" Kate asked, relieved.

"Nope. Just plant your pretty little butt on a stool over there and keep me company while I create magic." He gave his sauce another stir, then turned. "Oh, wait, I know one thing you can do. Go pick out something from the wine fridge and open it. I know we should probably do red since we're having red sauce, but screw that, I'm kind of in the mood for white if you're okay with it."

"You mean white, um, wine?"

He grinned. "That's what we keep in the wine fridge. Weird, huh?" He gestured with his spoon, indicating a glass-fronted wine cooler built into the base of the massive kitchen island. "The opener's in the little box on the counter above it."

Kate stepped over and peered in through the clear door. There had to be several dozen bottles in there, corks facing out. "I don't really know anything about wine. Which one do you want?"

"Wine's wine. Just grab the one with the coolest label. Or close your eyes and point." Fitz shrugged. "My folks hire a sommelier to buy for them, so it should all be good."

Kate hesitated. She didn't normally drink wine. She didn't normally drink at all, aside from maybe a few sips of beer at a party or a taste of her dad's Scotch on Christmas. But Fitz was in such a good mood now—she didn't want to ruin it. Opening the door, she reached in through the rush of frosty air and grabbed the first pale-colored bottle she saw.

A few minutes later the food was ready. "Allow me," Fitz said, hurrying over to pull out Kate's chair.

"Thanks." Kate's stomach grumbled; she realized she'd forgotten to eat lunch. Oops. Good thing Tommi still wasn't back from Philadelphia.

"Bon appetit." Fitz reached for the wine bottle, pouring a generous amount into her glass before filling his own. "Let's eat."

Kate waited while he served them both some of the pasta. Then she twirled a few strands around her fork, blowing to cool it before popping it into her mouth.

"Wow," she said after chewing and swallowing. "This is really good!"

He grinned. "You don't have to sound so surprised. I may

not be able to ride worth a damn, but even a pathetic loser like me can open a jar of sauce."

"Stop. You know you ride great." Kate took another bite. This time she forgot to blow on it first, and it burned the roof of her mouth a little. She grabbed her wineglass and took a big drink to cool off. The wine tasted pretty good, too, sweet and a little spicy at the same time.

Fitz raised his own glass. "To us," he said.

Kate clinked her glass against his and smiled. "I'll drink to that." She took another small sip to prove it.

For the next few minutes they just ate and talked about this and that—Flame's training, the upcoming show, their friends. The food tasted good, and Kate started to relax and forget about their earlier sniping.

"Looks like you just about killed that spaghetti," Fitz said after a while. "How about seconds? There's plenty."

"Sure, just a little." Kate smiled as she realized she actually was still hungry. It was nice to have her appetite back. To feel so normal, sitting here having a good time with her boyfriend.

Fitz glanced at her. "What are you grinning about?"

"Nothing. Just happy to be here."

"Me too." He dumped more pasta on her plate, then stood and leaned across the table to kiss her.

"Hey!" she said, laughing. "You got sauce on my chin."

He grinned, dropping back into his chair and reaching for the wine bottle. "Sorry. Here, drink this—that'll make you forget what a hopeless oaf I am."

"No more for me." Kate reached out to block him from

refilling her glass, but it was too late. Her head already felt a little fuzzy, and no wonder. When had she gulped down almost the entire glass of wine?

Fitz was already topping off his own glass. "A toast," he said, raising it. "To my excellent cooking skills."

"To that." Kate clinked his glass, then took the tiniest sip she could. "And to your excellent modesty, too."

He laughed. "To both of us kicking ass at Washington Crossing."

That reminded Kate that the other grooms were probably still at the barn, preparing for the show. Banishing the thought, she quickly took another sip. "To Flame."

"For sure. And also, to Summer's over-the-top crazy Sweet Spoiled Sixteen bash," Fitz added with a grin. "Can't wait to see her ride in on an elephant dressed as Mickey Mouse or whatever."

Kate was already taking another sip, and she almost snorted the wine out through her nose. She couldn't seem to stop laughing.

"Summer won't really hire an elephant, will she?" she gasped out at last.

Fitz just grinned. "I guess we'll have to wait and see."

They continued to joke around as they finished their food. Finally Kate put down her fork. She'd forgotten to put her watch back on after showering, but she knew it had to be getting late.

"Um, so is it okay if I set the alarm for five thirty tomorrow?" she asked. "I want to be at the barn before seven if possible."

Fitz shrugged. "We can figure that out later. First we need to decide what to have for dessert. There's ice cream in the freezer, or—"

"It's okay, I'm stuffed." Kate pushed back from the table. "I couldn't eat another thing, seriously. I'll help you with the dishes, then I'd better get to sleep."

He reached over and grabbed her hand before she could stand up. "But it's still early!" he protested. "And we've hardly spent any time together today."

Was he kidding? Kate felt as if they'd been glued at the hip all day long.

"Sorry," she said softly. "I really need to get to bed, or I'll be dead on my feet tomorrow."

He pretended to pout for a moment, then shrugged and let go of her hand. "Okay. At least let me bring you a cup of tea?"

"Sure, okay." Kate was so relieved that he wasn't mad that she didn't argue, even though she never drank tea. She picked up her plate and silverware, but Fitz gently took them from her.

"Go get ready for bed," he insisted. "Just leave the dishes. Maid's coming tomorrow, so we don't have to worry about it."

Kate hesitated, glancing at the messy dishes, which she knew would be crusty and gross by morning. But she couldn't quite muster up the energy to protest, so she just nodded and headed down the hall toward her bedroom.

She realized she must have had more of the wine than she'd thought when it took her three tries to get her foot through the leg of her shorty pajamas. Yeah, she was probably going to pay for that tomorrow.

But it was too late to worry about it. Slipping under the

covers, she yawned and did her best to ignore the way the room was spinning as she tried to calculate how late she could sleep and still be ready to leave on time. She was fiddling with the alarm clock when a soft knock came on the door.

"Come in," she called.

Fitz entered, holding a steaming cup of tea. "There you go," he said, setting it down on the bedside table. "Room service."

"Thanks." Kate felt self-conscious as she noticed his eyes straying toward her pajama top. She tugged at the neckline, making sure it wasn't slipping down too much. "Good night."

"That's all I get?" Fitz's voice was suddenly soft and husky. "No good-night kiss?"

Kate's heart pounded as he bent toward her, planting one hand on either side of her body as he kissed her. A moment later she felt the mattress sink on one side as he swung one knee onto the bed beside her.

"Wait," she said, struggling to focus through the fog in her mind. To figure out what was happening here. "We shouldn't—"

"It's okay." His eyes locked on hers. "We're just saying good night."

She turned her head to avoid another kiss. "You should, um, probably go."

"What's the matter?" He sounded kind of hurt now. "Don't you trust me?"

"Sure," she said. "I mean, of course. I mean—"

"It's okay." He traced her collarbone with one finger. "Can't I just hold you while you fall asleep? Please?"

"Um . . ." Kate's cloudy mind couldn't seem to come up with a response to that. Besides, how could she say no? He'd been so sweet all weekend. And he knew she didn't want things to go too far. They'd worked that all out after that awkward evening in the hay stall. She *did* trust him not to push her again, didn't she?

Before she quite knew how it had happened, Fitz was lying beside her, his long legs under the covers. He slid one arm around her shoulders. "There," he whispered. "That's nice."

Kate could feel his warm breath on her neck and his cold foot snaking up over her bare legs. Then they were kissing again, and Fitz's free hand was wandering, and suddenly Kate got a weird, out-of-body feeling—as if she were floating up above the bed looking down at herself. Herself in bed with Fitz, the guy who'd already bedded half the A circuit. The guy who now said he was her boyfriend, that he was willing to wait. But was he really? He was used to having girls say yes to him. A chilly trickle of panic ran through her as she realized how easily he could overpower her if he wanted to—would he really stop if she said no?

"Get off of me!" she blurted, shoving herself to a sitting position so fast that her shoulder banged into the side of his face. "This—we—I said you should go!"

Fitz drew back, looking surprised. "Kate—" he began.

"I mean it!" Kate's voice shook. "You need to leave now."

He frowned, shimmying away from her and standing up. "Fine." His voice was clipped. "Good night, I guess."

Without another word, he hurried out, closing the door behind him. It wasn't quite a slam, but almost.

Kate just sat there for a moment, still shaking. Then she

climbed out of bed and tiptoed over to the door. She listened for a moment, trying to tell if there was anyone on the other side. Then, as quietly as she could, she clicked the little button to lock it.

FOURTEEN

— — — — —

"Where's my plaid bag?" Court called, her voice echoing due to her head being halfway into the trunk of Abby's car.

"Right here." Tommi grabbed the bag off the sidewalk and brought it over. "Wow, the trunk looks so empty now without Brooke's stuff."

"I know!" Brooke wailed. She was standing at the bottom of the steps of her cousin's off-campus house, both arms wrapped around herself, looking pitiful. "I can't believe you guys are leaving already! I want to throw my bags back in the car and go home to New York with you."

"No, you don't," Mariah told her. "You're going to have a blast here."

"Yeah. By next weekend you'll probably forget we even exist." Abby shrugged. "And who can blame you? The guys here make high school guys look like kindergartners."

"That's because the guys at our school *act* like kinder-gartners." Court glanced at Tommi. "Hey, with all this extra space where Brooke's stuff was, maybe you can squeeze in a souvenir from your visit to Penn," she teased. "Like, say, a certain gorgeous dreadlocked dude?"

"Shut up." Tommi shot a look toward the house, but Jon and Rashad were inside, printing out directions for the trip home.

Mariah shoved another suitcase into the trunk. "Yeah," she said. "There might even be room left over for that adorkable nerdboy you picked up the other day, Tommi."

This time Tommi just smiled. She was really glad she'd come on this trip. The lecture on ancient Egypt had been interesting, and the guy she'd gone with had turned out to be funny and smart and okay, maybe a little dorky, but in a cool way. Tommi had spent more than an hour chatting with him over coffee after the lecture before her friends had finally called her away for dinner. That evening all five girls had gone barhopping around campus and eventually joined up with Jon and Rashad and some of their friends at another party, this one at someone's friend-of-a-friend's off-campus house. On Sunday the girls had slept in, then had brunch, followed by a full afternoon of shopping in other parts of the city. Later they'd met up with Jon and Rashad again and the whole group had gone to a music club to see a local band. As she'd swayed to the music, Tommi had thought of Alex—and realized it was the first time all day that she'd done so. She knew he'd love the club, which was small and quirky and very un–New York, though she couldn't quite manage to wish that he was there.

Monday was turning out to be another gorgeous, perfect late-summer day. Tommi and her friends had spent the morning hanging out on campus, then gone to lunch with the guys. Now it was time to leave Philadelphia and campus life and head home to New York.

Tommi tossed the last of her bags into the trunk, then checked her purse to make sure her phone was inside. It now held the names, numbers, and e-mail addresses of several new guys, including Rashad. She wasn't sure she'd ever use them, but that really wasn't the point. She'd enjoyed getting to know a bunch of new people. Okay, so she still felt a twinge of guilt when she thought about Alex. What would he say if he knew what she'd been up to this weekend?

But she shrugged that off. They'd only been together for a month or so. They'd never even really talked about being exclusive. So what was the big deal?

"Is that everything?" Mariah asked, stepping back from the trunk and glancing around for stray bags.

"Think so." Abby slammed it shut. "We should hit the road. I told my folks I'd be home before dark. They're totally paranoid about me driving in the city at night."

There was a flurry of hugs and tears as they all said goodbye to Brooke. "I wish you guys could stay!" she wailed, her voice muffled by being buried in Tommi's shoulder.

"Me too," Tommi said, almost meaning it.

She was glad she'd come. She loved riding and showing and everything else about her life. That didn't mean it wasn't nice to have a break from it once in a while, try something different. This had been one of those times, one of those perfect weekends that took her out of her real life in just the right way. Yes, she almost hated to head back.

Almost.

"Easy, big fella," the farrier murmured as the horse he was trimming shifted its weight.

Kate blinked, realizing her mind had drifted as she held the horse's lead rope. She clucked to it, giving a light tug on the lead to make sure its focus stayed on her.

The farrier, Burt, finished with the hoof and straightened up. "That all for today?" he asked, giving the horse a pat.

"What?" Kate said. "Um, I mean yeah. I mean I'm not sure. I mean, I'd better check with Joy."

Burt tilted his head and studied her. "You okay, Katie? You look like you're a million miles away."

"Sorry. I mean I'm fine." Kate shrugged. "Just busy—you know, Washington Crossing and all . . ."

She let her voice trail off as she led the horse away down the aisle. The truth was, she'd been distracted all day. She couldn't seem to stop thinking about what had happened—and what had *almost* happened—between her and Fitz last night. Had she overreacted? Fitz certainly seemed to think so. He'd apologized that morning for being pushy again, but things had seemed a little frosty between them even after that. Instead of driving her to the barn himself, he'd called a car service to take her.

"My treat, obviously," he'd said, not quite meeting her eye. "But I mean, I'm not really supposed to show up there today anyway, right? This way I don't have to listen to some lecture from Jamie about the definition of the phrase 'closed on Mondays.'"

Kate had forced a laugh, and Fitz had kissed her on the forehead as she'd left. But still, things felt different.

She deposited the freshly shod horse in his stall, then stood there staring at him without really seeing him. Fitz had stepped in to help her when she was desperate. He hadn't done a thing wrong since then except want to spend time with her and be close to her. And all she seemed able to do was confuse him or piss him off.

Was she screwing up the best thing that had ever happened to her?

Zara checked the clock on the wall for the millionth time. Almost two thirty.

"If Gina doesn't get back soon, she's going to miss her freaking plane," she muttered to the empty loft.

She drummed her fingers on the coffee table, debating whether to call her mother's cell to see what was up. She'd spent the morning coming up with one last story to explain away Stacie's absence. Now all she wanted was to get it over with. Pack Gina off to the airport, then scoot up to Central Park to meet Marcus.

Marcus. A smile spread over Zara's face as she picked up her cell phone, scrolling down to the text he'd sent her about getting together today. She couldn't wait to see him again. Would he seem as hot and mysterious the second time around? Either way, getting to know him better would be a good way to celebrate surviving the past week.

Then a thought occurred to her. Her mother was notorious for always running late. What if she'd overslept out in the Hamptons and had to rush straight to the airport instead of coming back to the loft? If that was the case, Zara might not even need her cover story.

Before she could get too excited about that, she heard a flurry of footsteps clickety-clacking along in the hallway outside. She dropped her phone on the coffee table, then rushed over and flung open the door.

"You'll never guess what happened," she began.

Her mother breezed into the apartment and dropped her overnight bag on the floor. "No wait, me first," she exclaimed. Her cheeks were flushed, and her eyes sparkled. "I talked to my agent and things are still up in the air on set, so I decided to change my plans. I'm staying another week!"

"What?" For a second Zara wasn't sure she'd heard her right. "What do you mean, you're staying?"

Gina bustled over and planted a kiss on Zara's cheek. "There's no point in going back to Vancouver just to stand around when I could be watching my lovely and talented daughter ride in her big show this weekend, right?" She stepped back and clapped her hands like a little kid. "I can't wait! It's been too long since I've gotten to see you ride, love."

She sounded excited, but Zara's heart sank like a stone. Now what?

Gina stepped over to glance at the answering machine, then looked around the main room. "Where's Stacie?" she asked. "I'm looking forward to having more than an hour or two to get to know her."

Zara gulped. "Um, that's what I was about to tell you. She's not here."

"Oh?" Gina raised one perfectly groomed eyebrow. Was that a look of suspicion in her expressive brown eyes?

But Zara couldn't worry about that. She was in too deep now.

"Yeah." She picked at a loose thread on the arm of the sofa. "It's because of her old childhood piano teacher, I think. Anyway, some old dude who lives in Boston. Zac might know who I mean. Someone called first thing this morning and said he got rushed to the hospital."

"Oh, dear."

Zara couldn't tell whether her mother was buying it so far or not. "Anyway, Stacie hopped the first train up to see him." She shrugged. "She was planning to come back tonight so I wouldn't be here alone. But now that you're sticking around, maybe I'll text her and let her know she can stay if she wants. That's okay, right?"

Gina kicked off her shoes and wriggled her toes. She studied Zara's face for a long moment. Zara held her breath. Had she sold it? Or was her whole story about to come crashing down?

"Of course," Gina said at last. "Please let her know I—"

The buzz of Zara's cell phone cut her off. Zara grabbed it, her mind immediately jumping to Marcus.

"Hang on, I need to check this," she told her mother. "I'm supposed to be meeting a friend at the park in a while."

"Fine." Gina hurried off into the kitchen as Zara read the text.

hi Zara, I just wanted to make sure u aren't going to tell anyone about that pic u saw. Pls? I'm srs, u can't tell ANYONE. OK? text me back if u want. yr friend, Summer

Zara rolled her eyes. Definitely *not* Marcus.

"How the hell'd Summer get my number?" she muttered under her breath. The girl was seriously whacked out. But she didn't have time to worry about Summer's petty little problems right now. Or ever, really. But *especially* right now.

Gina stepped back into the room, holding a bottle of spring water. "Everything okay with your friend?" she asked.

"Huh? Oh, sure." Zara slipped the phone into the pocket of her shorts. "That was him—he's already on his way to the park. So I'd better scoot."

"Him?" Gina smiled. "Anyone I should know about?"

Zara grabbed her purse off the sofa. "Just a friend. No biggie." She headed for the door, then paused. "Oh, and don't worry, I'll text Stacie in the cab, okay?"

"All right. Have a nice time. Can we have dinner tonight?"

"Yeah, sounds good. See you later."

Zara rushed out of the loft. She wasn't actually supposed to meet Marcus for a couple of hours, but suddenly she really needed to get away. Partly so Gina wouldn't ask any difficult questions before Zara worked out how to handle this new twist.

But mostly so she could figure out why she actually felt a teensy bit . . . *guilty* about lying to her mother.

Since when had that sort of thing bothered her?

FIFTEEN

"Good boy," Kate murmured as Flame moved sideways at a nudge from her outside leg. She was practicing the lateral work he'd learned so far, and he was doing great. "Such a smart guy!"

The horse's left ear flicked back toward her, then a moment later swiveled along with the right one, aiming toward the edge of the ring. Kate glanced that way and her heart let out a thump. Fitz was leaning on the rail, watching her.

What's he doing here? she thought, various possibilities skittering through her mind before she could stop them. He'd come to break up with her. He wanted to tell her off for leading him on last night . . . She shoved those thoughts aside quickly, not wanting her anxiety to transfer to the horse.

Not that that was a big issue with Flame. So far he was turning out to have the perfect temperament for a show hunter—calm and easygoing without being dull.

She sent him into a trot, then risked one more glance over

at Fitz. He caught her eye this time, waving and shooting her a thumbs-up.

"He's looking good!" he called.

Kate circled around to where he was standing, then asked Flame to halt. The gelding responded immediately, halting squarely right beside Fitz, then immediately snaking his head over to mug for treats.

"Heya, dude." Fitz dug a peppermint out of his pocket and held it out. The big D-shaped rings of the horse's bit clanked as he chewed the treat. Meanwhile Fitz looked up at Kate. "Having fun up there?"

Kate shot him a quick smile, then hid her discomfort by leaning forward to give Flame a pat. "Yeah, he's doing great," she said. "Um, I didn't think you were coming up to the barn today. Closed on Mondays, remember?"

"Just call me a rebel. If Jamie tells me I can't ride on Mondays, then dammit, that's when I want to ride!" He grinned. "No, seriously, I just came to pick you up."

Kate wasn't sure how to respond. He was acting as if nothing was wrong, as if last night hadn't happened. What did that mean?

At that moment Flame shifted his weight, giving her an excuse to focus on him. "I'll be done here pretty soon," she said. "I just want to school him a little more while we've got the ring to ourselves."

"Take your time. I'll just hang here and enjoy the view."

That was the sort of thing he said all the time. She'd almost learned to ignore those comments, take them as just Fitz being Fitz. This time, though, she found herself blushing the way she had at the beginning, when he'd first started paying attention to her.

As she sent Flame into a brisk trot, she did her best to return her focus to her riding. It actually worked, mostly—so much so that she was startled when she pulled up fifteen or twenty minutes later and saw that Jamie had joined Fitz at the rail.

"Nice work, Kate," the trainer called as she rode over. "He's really coming along."

"Thanks." Kate gave Flame a scratch on the withers. "He's a fast learner."

Jamie nodded, then turned to Fitz. "Have to admit I was skeptical about taking him to the show this week," he said. "But I think you're right. He's ready."

"Cool." Fitz grinned. "Am I allowed to say I told you so?"

"No." Jamie shot him a look. "And don't get too excited. I didn't say he's ready to show. He could still use a little more weight, for one thing. And obviously the options are limited until we get him jumping. But we can let him hang out and get used to the atmosphere, do some schooling in the mornings. Play the rest by ear. Maybe think about an eq on the flat class or something to test the waters toward the end of the week if he's doing well."

"Sounds like a plan."

Kate was trying to catch up. "Wait," she said. "Are you guys talking about Flame? Like, taking him to Washington Crossing?"

Jamie glanced up at her and nodded. "Fitz has been harassing me about it all weekend. I have to admit I wasn't convinced at first, but seeing him go just now, I see no reason to put it off."

"Are you sure?" Kate blurted out. She didn't normally talk back to Jamie or question his training decisions. But this time, she couldn't help it. "I mean, he's barely been off the track a month!"

Jamie chuckled. "Not exactly."

"Yeah." Fitz reached over the fence to give Flame a pat. "I meant to tell you, Kate. Joy talked to Mr. Tanner yesterday— she called to ask him a few questions for our boy's file, like when he'd been dewormed last and stuff like that. So you know how chatty Joy is, I guess the two of them hit it off over the phone and he talked her ear off, giving her Flame's whole backstory." He shrugged. "Let's just say it's not quite the same as Nat's version."

"What do you mean?" Kate looked from Fitz to Jamie and back again.

"Flame's been off the track longer than Nat told us," Fitz said. "The Tanners got him from some guy who picked him up from Finger Lakes like last November or something. He turned him out for the winter, then the Tanners bought him this summer."

Kate wasn't sure what to say. She knew Nat was prone to exaggeration, but she couldn't believe she'd lied about this. Or wait—maybe she could. Nat always acted as if she didn't care what anyone thought of her. But somehow, her stories always seemed to involve herself doing something super amazing. Hooking up with the hottest guy at the party. Telling off some annoying teacher in the most clever and snarky way ever.

Scoring the biggest bargain at the mall. And now, riding the toughest, hottest, straight-off-the-trackiest horse in the barn. Come to think of it, maybe Kate *could* believe it.

Jamie checked his watch. "Too bad whoever had him didn't put more weight on him over the winter. But I'm sure we'll have him looking like a show horse in no time. I'll let Miguel know he's tagging along when we leave for Washington Crossing in the morning."

"Thanks." Fitz lifted his hand in a lazy wave as the trainer hurried off. Then he turned to Kate. "I'll help you put him away so we can get out of here."

It took Kate a moment to hear him as she slid down from the saddle and ran up her stirrups. She was still taking in what she'd just learned. Once again, Nat had managed to take her in, make her feel like an idiot . . .

"Wait, what?" she said, glancing over at Fitz as his words finally sank in. "I can't leave yet. I still have a ton to do."

"Oh, really? Maybe *this* will change your mind." Fitz reached into his pocket and pulled out two slips of colorful paper, which he waved in Kate's face. "Check it out—I scored a couple of awesome seats for that Broadway show we were talking about the other night!" He checked his watch. "Actually, we're going to have to book to make it by curtain time."

Kate pushed Flame's nose aside as the horse reached out and tried to nibble on the tickets. "What?" she said. "Are you serious?"

"Would I lie to you?" He stuck the tickets back in his pocket. "Come on, maybe we can find one of the grooms to untack for us."

Kate's fingers clenched around the reins. How could she say no when Fitz was being so sweet and romantic? This was the kind of thing other girls swooned over. And Kate was feeling a little swoony herself. More than a little relieved, too. Whatever that had been last night, Fitz seemed to be over it.

"Yo, Javier!" Fitz called, taking a few quick steps toward the barn and waving his arms over his head.

Kate glanced over just in time to see the young groom rushing past just inside the big double doors, which were standing open to catch any hint of a breeze. Javier's arms were full of fleece saddle pads, and a bucket was dangling from his elbow.

"Guess he didn't hear me," Fitz muttered with a shrug as Javier disappeared without slowing down.

Kate gulped. Seeing Javier had just brought her back to reality. They were leaving for Washington Crossing first thing in the morning, and there were still a million things to do before then.

"I'm sorry," she told Fitz. "I can't go tonight."

Fitz spun to face her. "Huh?"

"I can't go to that Broadway play." Kate took a deep breath, forcing herself to meet his eye. "You know we're leaving for the show in the morning. I can't stick the other guys with my share of the work." *Especially since you made me leave early last night*, she added in her mind, though she didn't say it out loud.

Fitz stared at her. "Come on," he said. "You're a working student, not a paid employee. I'm sure Jamie doesn't expect you to—"

"I'm sorry," Kate broke in. Fitz could argue his way into or out of just about anything, and she didn't want to let him get started. For one thing, she didn't have the time. "It's really sweet of you to get those tickets, but I really can't. Not tonight."

He frowned. "Give me a break, Kate. I'm trying to make this work. Can't you even meet me halfway here?"

"I'm sorry," Kate said again. "But I have a job here. I can't just run off and dump the work on everybody else whenever I feel like it."

"Okay, this again." Fitz rolled his eyes. "Don't think I'm too stupid to read between the lines. You basically think I'm just some spoiled rich kid who doesn't care about anything. Have I got that about right, Miss Too Good for You?"

"No!" Kate blurted out. "That's not what I said at all. But not everyone can afford to be impulsive all the time like you."

"And not everyone wants to be uptight all the time like you," he shot back. "I don't know why I bother sometimes. I try to do something nice for you, plan a fun evening to make up for last night, whatever the hell *that* was—"

Kate winced as if he'd struck her. So *that's* what this was about?

"Just so you know," she said through clenched teeth, willing her voice not to shake, "it doesn't always work. Your stupid grand gestures can't always solve everything."

"Fine. Then I won't waste them on you anymore." Fitz turned away and pulled out his phone. He punched in a number and pressed the phone to his ear.

Kate just stood there, still holding Flame's reins, not sure what to do. Was their fight over? Who was he calling?

"Hey, Sharon," Fitz said into the phone, his voice suddenly light and jovial again. How did he *do* that? "It's Fitz Hall.

How've you been? Listen, are you busy tonight? Because I've got a couple of tickets for—"

That was all Kate heard. "Come on, boy," she whispered, pulling Flame along with her toward the barn before Fitz could see her burst into tears.

"Two, please," Marcus told the hot dog vendor. He glanced at Zara. "You want mustard, or what?"

"Just ketchup on mine." Zara shot him a sidelong look. "Mustard is the food of the devil."

Marcus smiled. "Whatever you say."

Soon they were sitting on a park bench chowing down on their hot dogs. The sun was sinking lower over the Upper West Side skyline, casting welcome shade over the park.

Zara was having a great time. She couldn't believe how well she and Marcus clicked. He just seemed to *get* her. They'd been wandering around the park for the past half hour, talking and getting to know each other a little better. Best of all? He looked even more adorable in jeans and a T-shirt than he had all dressed up for the movie premiere.

"So when are you leaving for your horse show again?" he asked, licking mustard off his finger.

"Not until Friday. My horses are going down tomorrow with the barn, though. My trainer's going to take my hunter mare in a couple of schooling classes to prep her for me." Zara shot him a look. "Wait, sorry for the horsey lingo. A mare is a female horse, and—"

"Yeah, I know, I get it," he cut her off with a smile. "I'm not a complete idiot when it comes to horses. Used to ride some when I was younger, remember?"

"Oh, yeah." Zara vaguely recalled that he'd mentioned that when they'd first met. "Down in Texas, right? English or Western?"

"Little of both." He reached over and flicked away a leaf that had fallen onto her knee. His fingers grazed her bare leg, and Zara shivered. "But I'm boring. Finish telling me about your show. Does your trainer ride your horses for you a lot?"

Zara shoved the last bite of her hot dog into her mouth to avoid answering for a second. Was this dude for real? Usually the guys she met loved to talk about themselves. Even Tommi's pal Grant, who was nicer than most. It was all about how hot *he* was for her, how much *he* wanted to touch her, how she made *him* feel, blah blah blah.

But Marcus? Totally different. All he wanted to talk about was Zara. And not in the way her parents' groupies did, either. Like Tommi's annoying boyfriend Alex, for example, who was always trying to pump Zara for info on Zac. No, Marcus seemed to want to hear about *her*. What she liked, what she did, who she was. It was kind of weird, but also kind of awesome.

She chewed and swallowed, then glanced at him. He was watching her. Waiting to hear what she had to say. What the hell? Zara decided to go with it.

"Jamie doesn't ride my jumper much," she told him, wiping her fingers on a napkin and then standing to toss it in a nearby bin. "But he rides Ellie—that's my mare—quite a bit."

Marcus stood, too, and they started wandering down the dappled path again. "Oh yeah? Why the difference?"

"Well, for one thing I haven't had Ellie as long. Plus she's a little, um, spicier than Keeper." Zara grinned as she thought back on some of the opinionated mare's antics since the two of them had become a team. "Actually, I should probably be up at the barn riding her right now. With my mom in town I haven't had much time to ride lately, and Ellie's been pretty fresh. I'll be lucky if she doesn't buck me off over the first fence on Friday."

Marcus chuckled. "Sounds exciting."

"Yeah. But that's okay—I live for excitement." On impulse, she reached over and grabbed his hand. He shot her a surprised look, then squeezed back.

They walked along like that for a moment, hand in hand, not talking. They were nearing the edge of the park at Fifth Avenue, and Zara could hear the growl of traffic growing louder with every step. However, the spot they were in right now was deserted except for a couple of squirrels chasing each other around up in one of the trees.

She pulled him to a stop and turned to face him. "So enough about me," she said. "Tell me more about you. How'd you end up at that movie premiere, anyway?"

He smiled down at her, his dark eyes suddenly going all intense. "Guess it must've been fate." He lifted his free hand, brushing back her hair.

Zara held her breath as their eyes locked. She was tempted to just throw herself at him, but she held back. It never hurt to play a little hard to get. Guys liked that.

He ran his hand down her arm, stopping somewhere around her elbow. Zara knew a moment when she found herself in one. And this was definitely a moment. But just as he started to pull her toward him, there was a loud buzz from Zara's pocket.

"Crap," she blurted out. "That's my phone." She yanked it out and quickly turned off the ringer. "Now where were we?"

But it was too late; he was already stepping away. "It's okay, go ahead and get it if you want."

Just like that, the moment was gone. Double crap. Zara glanced at the phone. "It's nothing important. Just another stupid text from freaking Summer."

"Who?"

"Just this girl at my barn." Zara scanned the text. Same old, same old. "I saw this photo on her e-mail and she wants me to swear, like, a blood oath that I'll never tell anyone about it."

"Really?" Marcus raised his eyebrows. "Scandalous?"

Zara rolled her eyes. "Hardly. It's just an old picture of her from when she was a little kid. I guess back then her ears stuck out, like, freakishly far."

"Back then?" He looked confused.

"Yeah. See, in this picture I saw, she was wearing a riding helmet and had her hair pulled back, so it was kind of hard to miss, you know? So she starts freaking out and begging me not to tell anyone, because she had some kind of plastic surgery to fix it on her tenth birthday, and nobody she hangs out with now even knows about it."

"Oh. Weird."

"Tell me about it." Zara kicked at a stone on the path.

Leave it to Summer to make some huge freaking deal about this. Just like she was making a huge freaking deal about her stupid party. "Hey, that reminds me," she said. "Crazy Summer's having a big Sweet Sixteen bash this Friday night. Want to go with me?"

"Friday?" Marcus shrugged. "I'll have to check. Let you know in a day or two?"

Zara held back a smile. So now *he* was the one playing hard to get, huh? Good. She liked a challenge.

"Sure, let me know." She sidled closer, slipping both arms around his waist. "I'm sure we'd have a lot of fun. Here's a little preview . . ."

She stood on tiptoes, and a moment later they were kissing. His lips were warm, his face scratchy with stubble. Zara shivered as his hands ran down her back.

Before she could push things any further, though, he pulled away. "That was nice," he said. "But listen, I've got to go." He checked his watch. "Let me grab you a cab, okay?"

"What? But we just got here," Zara complained, her entire body still tingling from the kiss.

"Sorry." He was already hurrying ahead toward the street. By the time Zara caught up, a taxi was zigzagging its way over through the steady stream of traffic. Marcus leaned down and kissed her lightly, then opened the back door. "I'll call you soon."

Zara wasn't sure what to do other than climb into the cab. "Where to?" the cabbie asked without turning around.

"SoHo," Zara said, giving the address. She turned to look out the window, but Marcus was already hurrying away up the street. "What the hell was *that* all about?" she muttered, feeling intrigued and annoyed and turned on and confused all at the same time.

Tommi let her eyes drift shut as she sank lower in the tub. It was only a little after seven, but she was already looking forward to a good night's sleep. The weekend had been fun but exhausting, and she needed to be back on her game for her first classes at Washington Crossing tomorrow afternoon.

She was sinking deeper into the bubbles when she heard her cell phone buzz. It was sitting on the edge of the sink, which was way too far to reach from the tub. She almost let the call go to voice mail, but then realized she hadn't spoken to Alex since returning from Philadelphia. Might as well get it over with, or he'd be texting and calling all evening.

Climbing to her feet, she stepped out of the tub with one foot and lunged across the bathroom to grab the phone, slinging water and jasmine-scented bubbles all over the place.

"Dammit," she muttered as the phone almost slid out of her wet hand. She managed to catch it and punched the button to answer without checking to see who was calling. "Hello?"

"Hi, this is Adam Dane," a male voice said. "Is this Tommi Aaronson?"

Tommi squeezed her eyes shut. This she didn't need right now. She perched on the edge of the tub, which felt cold, hard, and slippery against her skin.

"Uh, yes, hi," she said, doing her best to sound mature and businesslike. "This is Tommi. How are you?"

"Fine, fine. Listen, your barn's going to Washington Crossing, right? Thought maybe I could bring my client to see that horse of yours down there."

"Oh! Sure, that sounds fine . . ." Tommi went on to set up an appointment time for the next afternoon, then said goodbye and hung up.

She sat there staring at the phone for another moment, ignoring the clumps of bubbles sliding down her legs. Tomorrow. She had to show Legs tomorrow, even though she hadn't ridden him in five days. How was she going to pull that off? For a second she was tempted to call Adam Dane back and see if he could reschedule for later in the week.

But she could almost hear her father chiding her: *A delayed sale is a lost sale, Thomasina.*

Tommi grimaced, banishing the thought. Her father was a businessman—one of the best in the world, according to a lot of people. But that didn't mean he knew anything about selling horses. He didn't understand that it was a lot different from selling a pair of shoes or something. Had this deal with him been a big mistake?

The phone rang in her hand, startling her. "Hello?" she barked out, slapping it to her wet cheek.

Once again, she hadn't checked the caller ID. She was expecting to hear Adam Dane again—maybe wanting to push back their appointment, if she was lucky.

Instead, Alex's voice spoke into her ear. "Hey, Tommi. Welcome home!"

"Alex!" Tommi closed her eyes for a moment, shifting gears. "Hey. I was going to call you later."

"So how was the big college weekend?"

"Pretty cool. We had fun, hit some parties, you know."

"Cool. Hey, speaking of fun parties, I checked out this new music club over the weekend and—"

He was off and running, describing the awesome new band he'd seen on Saturday night. Or something like that, anyway. Tommi wasn't really in the mood.

"Listen, that's great," she broke in after a moment. "But I'm kind of in the middle of something, so—"

"Oh! Okay, I'll let you go," Alex said. "But maybe we can get together later. You have dinner yet?"

"Tonight?" Tommi hesitated, wondering if she should go. She wouldn't have the chance to see Alex again until Summer's party. But even thinking about getting dressed and heading back out tonight made her feel more exhausted than ever. "Um, I can't," she said. "Sorry. But I'll see you at that party on Friday night, right?"

"For sure. See you then."

Tommi said good-bye and hung up. Alex sounded a little disappointed, but she figured he'd live. With a yawn, she tossed the phone aside and then slipped back into the rapidly cooling water.

SIXTEEN

----- ----- ----- ----- -----

The first day of a show was always a nonstop zoo. Especially a big, prestigious show like Washington Crossing. Pelham Lane's block of temporary tent stalls had to be checked for hazards, then the horses settled in, water buckets hung and filled, tack room set up, feed stall stocked . . . Kate felt as if she hadn't stopped moving since the trailers had pulled into the parking area that morning. And as far as she was concerned, that was just as well. The harder she worked, the less time and energy she had to think about other things.

She was giving the aisle a quick sweep when Tommi hurried in, car keys in hand and a large hobo bag slung over her shoulder. "Hey, Kate," Tommi said. "How's it going? Sorry I'm late; there was crazy traffic at the tunnel."

"Oh." Kate brushed a sweaty strand of hair out of her face, then glanced at her wrist. It was bare; she'd misplaced her watch somewhere along the way. Probably when she'd taken it off to give Jamie's Grand Prix horse a bath earlier. "Um, hi. What time is it?"

"Little before two. Are you okay?" Tommi peered at her. "You look kind of pale. Did you eat lunch?" She dug into her purse and pulled out a small bag of pretzels.

Kate took a deep breath, maybe the first she'd taken all day. "Thanks," she said, accepting the pretzels. "Actually, things have been a little crazy lately." Her lower lip trembled.

Tommi noticed. "You mean the usual show stuff?" she asked. "Or something else?"

Kate glanced at her bare wrist again. Force of habit. "Both, I guess," she said. "But I can't really talk right now—somebody needs to go lunge Mrs. Walsh's mare, and I—"

"It's okay. I just saw Miguel taking her out to the lungeing area." Tommi took Kate by the elbow and gently steered her into the tack stall, which was deserted except for Jamie's old bulldog, Chaucer, who was lounging in the wood chips. "So let's talk, okay?"

Kate was about to argue. But the concerned look in Tommi's eye reminded her that she was supposed to be leaning on her friend. Trusting her.

"Okay," she said softly, sinking down onto the edge of a monogrammed director's chair. "It's about Fitz . . ."

She went on to tell Tommi about their fight yesterday. And what had happened afterward. He'd sped off to meet "Sharon" for their Broadway date, leaving Kate uncertain what had just happened. But when a hired car had arrived an hour later to drop off the things she'd left at his apartment, she'd figured it out.

"So I guess we're, you know, broken up," she finished with a sniffle.

Tommi was scowling. "What an asshole," she said. "I mean, I always knew Fitz was a dog. But I thought . . ." She shook her head, her voice trailing off. "Never mind. Forget him. You're too good for him anyway. You did the right thing, Kate. Know that, okay?"

Kate just shrugged. "I guess. Anyway, I ended up staying at the barn late, then sneaking home to sleep. I don't think my parents even knew I was there."

At least that was one good thing. Another was that her brother had already been home and asleep when Kate had tiptoed in at midnight. There hadn't been any yelling, at least for the few hours Kate was there.

Tommi was digging into her shoulder bag. She pulled out something soft wrapped in a plastic bag and handed it to Kate.

"Here, this is for you," she said. "Sorry I didn't have time to gift-wrap it."

"What is it?" Kate opened the bag. When she saw what was inside, she gasped. "Breeches? But what—"

"Call it an early Christmas present." Tommi smiled. "Let me know if they fit—otherwise we can exchange them."

Kate couldn't speak for a moment, running her fingers over the little red and white Tailored Sportsman label on the side seam. Tommi was still the only one who knew about the disaster with old show breeches, though Kate had assumed her friend had forgotten that she still didn't have anything decent to wear. She should have known better.

"I shouldn't accept these," she said softly, admiring the fabric. "I cleaned up my schooling breeches well enough—I can just—"

"Forget it, I insist. The breeches are yours." Tommi hoisted her bag back up her shoulder. "Anyway, I'd better go. I'm supposed to show Legs to someone in like an hour, and I haven't even found his stall yet."

She hurried off before Kate could come up with a response.

Tommi was still thinking about what Kate had told her as she slipped the bit into Legs's mouth and buckled the noseband and throatlatch. She couldn't believe Fitz had dumped her. Well, okay, maybe she *could* believe it. He'd always had a short attention span when it came to girls. That didn't mean Tommi had to like it.

But she couldn't worry about it right now. She needed to focus. "Ready to go, boy?" she asked, giving the horse a pat on the shoulder. He jumped in surprise, almost breaking out of the cross-ties. Oops. He was pretty amped; she'd better get out there and start working him down.

She led him outside, giving him a chance to check out the surroundings as they walked around in search of a warm-up spot. The Washington Crossing show had one of the most picturesque settings of any A show on the East Coast. Hundreds of acres of rolling meadows and patches of forest surrounded a sprawling stone mansion. The showgrounds spilled out from the estate's original stableyard into several acres of what had once been pasture. It was a charming place to show, even if the parking area got muddy at the slightest hint of rain and the warm-up and lungeing areas were a hodgepodge of various fields, random open areas, and far too few actual rings with footing.

Twenty minutes into her warm-up, Tommi saw Adam Dane approaching the small, grassy turnout paddock behind the temporary barns that Tommi was using as a schooling ring. He was tall and tanned and blond, broad of shoulder but narrow everywhere else. Walking beside him was a middle-aged woman with an extra few pounds around the middle and a slightly nervous smile. Her boots and breeches looked brand-new and expensive.

"Hi." Tommi rode over to the fence. "Hope you don't mind trying him in here. All the rings are busy right now." She waved a hand at the line she'd set up in the middle of the paddock. "Someone left some jumps we can use."

"No problem." Adam looked Legs up and down. "Nice-looking animal. Just as Jamie described." He nodded toward the woman. "This is my student, Marie. She's been riding hunters for a while, and now she's looking for something to help her learn the ropes in the jumpers."

"Hello," Marie said. "He looks lovely."

"Hi." Tommi hesitated, shooting the client an uncertain smile before turning back to the trainer. "Maybe I wasn't clear enough on the phone," she said. "Legs has a lot of potential, but he's not exactly a schoolmaster type. He can be a tricky ride."

"Well, that's why she has a trainer, right, Marie?" Adam chuckled and patted the woman on the back. "Now let's see what he can do, all right?"

Tommi nodded. Marie didn't look like the kind of rider Legs needed. At all. Then again, looks could be deceiving. Maybe the woman was a more accomplished rider than she appeared. Otherwise, why would Adam bring her to see a horse like Legs? Tommi was sure Jamie had been honest when he'd described him.

With a cluck and a pulse of her calves, Tommi sent Legs into a trot. She spent a few minutes showing what he could do on the flat, then hopped him over the line of fences a couple of times before handing him over to Adam.

"He's a beautiful horse," the client said as Tommi joined her at the rail. "Adam thinks he could be just the thing for me."

"Hmm," Tommi said noncommittally. She held her breath as Adam swung into the saddle and Legs put his ears back and scooted forward. But the trainer settled him quickly, and proceeded to put Legs through his paces with little trouble.

"All right, Marie." He rode over on a loose rein, then jumped down and started adjusting the stirrups. "Want to give him a try?"

Marie ducked into the ring, then glanced around. "Is there a mounting block?" She tittered. "He's taller than my horse!"

"I don't think so, sorry," Tommi said. "Maybe Adam can give you a leg up?"

Legs tensed up again as the trainer hoisted the woman awkwardly into the saddle, where she immediately started fussing with the reins. "Take your time, Marie," Adam said, moving to the horse's head to take the reins from Tommi. "We don't have to do much on this first ride, all right?"

Finally the woman got herself organized. Adam stepped away, telling her to ask Legs for a walk.

Tommi winced as Marie booted the horse in the sides and he shot forward. "Easy with your legs," she called. "He's pretty responsive."

Adam shot her a look, then turned his attention back to his

client, who was hauling on the reins to stop the horse. "Relax, Marie," he called. "Just remember what we've been working on. Quiet hands, quiet legs. Now circle him around and see if you can get in sync with him."

Tommi barely dared to take a breath for the rest of the woman's ride. Fortunately it didn't last long. Adam had Marie do a few minutes of flatwork, then lowered one of the jumps, making it into a tiny crossrail which he had her canter Legs over a couple of times. The woman was just as novice as Tommi had guessed, if not more so, and Legs was clearly getting more confused by the moment.

"Good," Adam called as Legs cantered over the tiny jump, ears going back as the woman thumped down into the saddle afterward. "Pull him up. That was excellent."

"Okay," Tommi said, forcing a smile. "I guess it was worth a try, right?"

Adam glanced at her. "Hang tight, we should talk," he said. Then he stepped out to meet Marie and Legs, helping the woman down.

"He's probably a little much for me, I'm afraid," the woman told Tommi, huffing and puffing from the exertion of her short ride. "Don't you think so, Adam? He's a lovely horse, though."

"Thanks." Tommi took the horse from her and ran up the stirrups.

"If you don't like him, we'll keep looking," Adam told Marie smoothly. "But listen, I'll meet you back at the barn, all right? Tommi and I need to take care of some business." As soon as the woman was gone, he turned to Tommi. "Okay, let's talk price."

Tommi glanced up, startled. "What?" she blurted out.

"But I thought she decided to pass. They didn't really seem to be the best match."

Adam ignored that. "I'm sure there must be some wiggle room on the price you quoted me," he said. "I mean, the horse is clearly still green."

"Um, I don't know." Tommi was feeling a little blindsided. "I mean, everything's negotiable, but I really feel he's worth what I'm asking."

Adam shrugged. "The horse has got potential, sure. But you saw how difficult he was for Marie. I know you're new to this, but it's clear to me that he's a pro ride. Lucky for you, I kind of like him despite his issues. I'm willing to take a chance on him—for the right price, of course."

Tommi didn't respond for a moment. Now she got it. Adam was clearly hoping to pick up Legs at a bargain price, using his client's poor performance as an excuse. Hoping Tommi was naive and inexperienced enough to buy his story—to maybe even think he was doing her a favor. If Tommi fell for it, he'd probably be riding Legs in Grand Prix classes before the end of the summer, then selling him on for many times what he'd paid. Did he really think she was that stupid?

"He hasn't really been on the market that long." Tommi did her best to keep the annoyance out of her voice, though she wasn't sure she succeeded. "We've had some interest at full price, so—"

Adam rolled his eyes. "Look, I know your daddy's the hardball dealmaker of Wall Street, but cut me a break, okay, sweetheart? I'm just trying to make a living here. And we all know you don't really *need* to get full price, right?"

Tommi felt her cheeks go red. She was about to tell him exactly where to stick his obnoxious comments and shady business tactics. At that moment, though, she spotted Jamie hurrying past on the little gravel path leading toward the main ring area. He didn't see her, but seeing him made Tommi bite her tongue. Just as she knew he would do.

"Sorry," she said as politely as possible. "The price is firm."

He frowned. "Fine. Call me if you change your mind." Spinning on his heel, he hurried off without a backward glance.

Tommi spent the next few minutes walking Legs around the ring to cool him down, though she felt anything but cool herself. Was this crap really worth it?

The buzz of her phone interrupted her thoughts. It was Alex.

"Hey," he said when she answered. "How's the show going?"

"It's going." Tommi's voice came out sharper than she'd intended.

He didn't seem to notice. "Cool. So listen, I'm bummed we didn't get to hang out last night. And I'm not sure I can wait until Friday to see you again. How about if I drive down a day or two early? I swear I won't get in the way—I'll just watch you ride and cheer you on or whatever."

"Oh." Tommi couldn't help being flattered that he missed her so much. Her bad mood retreated, at least a little. "Um, are you sure you won't be bored? I won't have much time to hang out."

"That's okay." He paused. "So is your friend Zara riding in any of the same classes? Just wondering—she's fun to talk to."

Just like that, Tommi's bad mood came screaming back.

Yeah, that was just what she needed—Alex following Zara around, blabbing at her about how Zac Trask was some kind of musical genius, and Zara sniping at Tommi as a result.

"Listen, I just don't think it's a good idea," she said. "I'm going to be pretty busy for the rest of the week. You'd better just show up on Friday like we planned, okay? Anyway, I've got to go. Talk to you later."

She hung up before he could respond, not in the mood to deal with him anymore just then.

Zara scanned the Facebook photo album she'd just opened on her laptop, clicking on a sexy shot of herself in a bikini. She attached it to the e-mail she'd just typed up urging Marcus to say he'd come to Summer's party. It was Wednesday already, and he hadn't given her an answer yet. And after that delicious first kiss the other day, she didn't want to leave anything to chance. Hitting send, she waited for the e-mail to whoosh off into cyberspace and then smiled.

There. That should help convince him.

She glanced up, wincing, as her mother hit the high note in the octave she was do-re-mi-fa-so-ing. Or tried to hit it, anyway. Gina was having a singing lesson over by the piano at the opposite end of the loft. Her instructor, a pale-faced dude in his fifties who looked like the unholy offspring of a human and a ferret, just cleared his throat and told her to try again.

Zara returned her attention to her computer, idly wondering how the show was going so far. Most of the barn had gone down there yesterday, though Zara wasn't scheduled to show up until Friday, since her first classes were that afternoon.

Thinking about the show reminded her about that blog Summer had showed her. She ran a quick search and found it easily. *HORSESHOWSECRETS*, the headline read. *WHERE YOUR SECRETS ARE NEVER SAFE.*

She rolled her eyes. Pretty corny. She scrolled down past the latest few entries. There were five or six of them posted over the past couple of days—whoever was writing the blog had been pretty busy. But most of it was boring stuff involving people Zara didn't know at other East Coast barns.

Then her own name jumped out at her. She leaned closer, scanning the entry. It was pretty short:

Rumor has it that Zara Trask might be giving up on her spicy new hunter mare, Eleganz. Our sources say she's barely ridden the mare lately, instead letting superstar trainer Jamie Vos take over. Has the A circuit's own rock & roll wild child met her match?

"What?" Zara blurted out, reading through it again to make sure she wasn't seeing things. "Oh, *so* not cool!"

Gina broke off in mid-scale and glanced over. "What's that, love?" she called.

"Nothing." Zara glared at the screen. Who came up with this garbage? Was there a spy at Pelham Lane, or was some bored pony rider at another barn just making up random crap about strangers?

She noticed one more new entry below hers. Scrolling down, she realized this one was about Tommi. Something snarky about how "the circuit's brand-new billionaire horse trader" was so picky that she'd probably be stuck with her "so-called sales horse" forever.

Yikes, Zara thought. Tommi was going to flip out when she saw that.

She thought about forwarding it to her. Would Tommi appreciate that, or would she think Zara was just being obnoxious?

Before she could decide, the loft's main door flew open. Someone rushed in, sobbing loudly.

Zara jumped to her feet so fast she almost dropped her computer. "Stacie!" she blurted out.

SEVENTEEN

—— —— —— —— ——

Kate tensed when she heard a familiar laugh from just outside the tent where Pelham Lane's stalls were located. Fitz. She'd been wondering when he was going to turn up at the show. Now she knew—he was here.

She kept her head down, focusing on the bucket she was scrubbing. Would he act like everything was fine, the way he had the other time? Somehow she doubted it. It had been two days since he'd stormed off for his date with Sharon, and he hadn't so much as texted her.

A second later he rounded the corner. Kate stayed crouched over the water spigot, but she could see him out of the corner of her eye. And he wasn't alone. A girl was hanging off his arm, giggling and skipping and tossing her long honey-blond hair around.

Kate felt as if she'd been punched in the gut. She dumped the water out of the bucket she was working on, grabbed the two she'd already done, and took off around the corner without looking back. Had Fitz seen her? She hoped not, though she suspected she'd been hard to miss with her buckets clanking around.

Once she was out of sight in the next aisle she stopped, dropped the buckets, and just stood there trembling for a moment. She'd recognized the girl Fitz was with—her name was Hannah, and she was a Big Eq star from a prestigious A barn in northern New Jersey. She was one of the many girls Fitz had hooked up with before getting together with Kate, at least if you believed the rumors. And in this case? Kate did. Hannah was well known as a party girl.

She was also known as a pretty successful rider, making it as far as the first callback at the Maclay Finals last year. Kate couldn't argue with that kind of success, though secretly she found Hannah's riding a little pose-y and stiff. Her horse, a superpacker who was the veteran of countless medal finals himself, didn't seem to mind, and Kate had never seen the girl ride anything else, at least at a show.

But Hannah's riding wasn't the point. The point was, Fitz had already moved on, replaced Kate just as he'd replaced so many girls before when he got tired of them. Why had she thought she'd be any different?

"Oh, Fitz, you're here," Jamie's voice came from the next aisle, carrying easily to where Kate was standing. "I was just wondering if we'd have to scratch you from your classes this afternoon."

"I'm here," Fitz responded, sounding as carefree as ever. "And listen, slight change of plans."

"Oh?" Jamie sounded distracted. He always had a million things to do on show days.

"Yeah," Fitz went on. "You know Hannah, right?"

"Hi!" Hannah put in with a giggle.

Jamie didn't say anything. Kate could picture perfectly his quick, polite nod.

"So Hannah's agreed to catch-ride Flame for me during the show," Fitz said. "Just wanted to let you know."

"What?" Jamie sounded disapproving. "Where did this come from? I thought Kate was doing the riding."

"Yeah, she *was*." Fitz put a slight emphasis on the last word. "But as it turns out, she really doesn't have time this week. And I've got my hands full with my other horses. So—"

Kate didn't hear anything else as she grabbed her buckets and took off, half blinded by tears. So far she'd been so focused on the breakup itself that she hadn't really thought about the fact that Flame was Fitz's horse, not hers. Not *theirs*, as Fitz had tried to make her think. It hadn't even occurred to her when she'd hacked Flame around the show grounds yesterday afternoon, or taken him into one of the schooling rings that morning. The latter of which, she now realized, might have been her last ride on him ever.

Because it seemed she hadn't just lost Fitz. She'd lost Flame, too. One of the best horses she'd ever ridden, and now she wouldn't get to ride him anymore. Or help him develop into the show hunter he was born to be. Or pat his sleek red neck while watching the ringmaster pin a blue ribbon to his bridle . . .

Her stomach clenched as she suddenly understood exactly how Nat must be feeling right now. Which made her realize just how much she'd lost lately—her mother was slipping into crazy mode, her brother had turned into someone she didn't recognize, and now this.

All those things were out of her control. But there was one loss that might still be in her power to fix. Maybe it was time to suck it up and apologize to Nat, do her best to make things right with her. No guarantees that Nat would forgive her, of course, but at least she could try. She vowed to call or stop by her house as soon as she got home from the show. Now that this had happened, maybe she would even be able to convince Nat that she'd never meant to take Flame away from her. That she wouldn't wish this kind of pain on her worst enemy, let alone her best friend.

Okay, so it wasn't much of a silver lining. But it was the best Kate could come up with at the moment.

Zara was stunned as she stared at Stacie. Was this really happening?

Meanwhile Gina had stopped singing again. "Who's that?" she called from the far end of the room. "Did you say Stacie's back?"

Stacie herself didn't seem to notice anyone else was even in the loft. She'd stopped just inside the main room, flinging her bulging backpack onto a chair and then just standing there with her face buried in her hands, moaning and sobbing loudly.

Zara knew she had to do something. Now. Otherwise everything she'd worked so hard to build over the past week was going to come crashing down. Right on top of her.

She rushed over and grabbed Stacie in a big hug. "Welcome back, Stacie!" she said, loudly enough for her mother to hear. "How was Boston?"

Stacie barely seemed to hear her, though she hugged her back. "Oh, Zara!" she wailed. "You'll never believe what happened! Steve just totally broke my heart!"

Zara squeezed her tighter, leaning in until her mouth was about a quarter of an inch from Stacie's ear. "Shut up and listen to me," she hissed. "My mom's back, and she still believes you're actually a good babysitter. So play along unless you want your skinny white ass shipped back to nowheresville stat."

Stacie blinked, pulling away slightly. But she didn't say anything else. Zara had to hope that meant she'd caught on.

She turned to face her mother as Gina hurried over. "Look, Stacie's back from Boston," Zara told her. "Her old piano teacher, Steve, didn't make it. Did you just say he passed away this morning, Stacie?"

Stacie sniffled. "Um, yeah," she said. "This morning."

"Cousin Stacie. I'm so sorry for your loss." Gina reached out and clasped both of Stacie's hands in her own. "But it's good to finally meet you, even if it's under such tragic circumstances."

Zara almost rolled her eyes. Sure, Gina was probably being totally sincere. Too bad everything she said came out like a line in some sappy movie.

"You probably just need to sit down and chill for a while, right?" Zara tugged on Stacie's arm. "Come on, I'll help you bring your stuff upstairs."

"Yes, good idea," Gina said with another sympathetic smile. "Let me know if you need to talk, all right, dear?"

Stacie nodded and sniffled again, still looking a little confused. But Zara didn't give her a chance to answer. There was just one person Stacie needed to talk to right now, and that was her.

"Come on," she said, smiling through gritted teeth as she grabbed Stacie's bag. "Upstairs."

Tommi stepped into the tack stall. One of the younger grooms, Max, was in there hanging up a couple of ribbons someone had just won.

"Hi," Tommi greeted the groom. "Have you seen my gloves? I think I might have dropped them in here earlier."

Max tossed his thick reddish-brown hair out of his eyes. "Yeah, Miguel found them. I think he put them in there," he said in a voice that still showed a trace of an Irish accent, even though he'd lived in the States since he was nine years old. He pointed to the wooden tack trunk that served as a table.

"Thanks." Tommi picked up the framed photos that were sitting on top of the trunk and opened it. Her gloves were on the tray right inside the lid.

She was replacing the photos when she heard a loud shriek from just outside. Max glanced that way. "Sounds like Marissa," he commented.

"Better go see what's up." Tommi headed out of the tack stall and down the aisle. Right outside the entrance, she saw Marissa jumping up and down and hugging Dani, who was still on crutches.

"Hi," Tommi greeted Dani with a smile. "Couldn't stay away, huh?"

Dani laughed breathlessly and shoved Marissa away. "Quit,

before you knock me down and break the other leg," she told her. Then she glanced at Tommi. "Yeah, I'm going crazy with boredom just sitting around at home waiting for school to start."

"She's driving her parents crazy, too." Marissa giggled. "That's probably why they let her come."

Dani rolled her eyes. "Are you kidding? They knew they couldn't let me miss the party of the century." She glanced at Tommi. "And Marissa offered to let me share her hotel room, so they said I could come down a little early instead of moping around the house all week." She gave Marissa a nudge with the tip of her crutch. "We're going to have a blast!"

The two of them started chattering about Summer's party, but Tommi wasn't really listening anymore. She'd just spotted Fitz emerging from the barn. He was walking beside Elliot, who was leading Flame. The horse was tacked up and spit-shined to perfection, and the groom had a couple of rags sticking out of his pockets—the type they all carried for last-minute touch-ups to boots and bits. It looked as if they were heading off to the show ring. But that couldn't be right, could it?

"See you guys later, okay?" she said to Dani and Marissa. Then she hurried to catch up with Fitz. "Hey," she greeted him. "What's going on? Kate didn't tell me she's riding Flame in anything today."

Fitz looked over at her. "Kate's not riding Flame anymore."

"What?" Tommi glanced at Elliot, but the groom was fussing with the horse's bridle and didn't meet Tommi's eye. "What's that supposed to mean? She told me you guys had a fight or whatever, but—"

"Here I am! Wait up!" A girl raced out of the barn, almost crashing into Tommi as she headed for Fitz. "Okay, I found my helmet, thank God. So let's do this. Oh! Hi, Tommi."

"Hi, Hannah." Tommi was confused. She knew Hannah, of course—everyone on the circuit did. The girl was pretty much the exact opposite of a shrinking violet. She'd hung out with every girl and made out with every guy at barns up and down the East Coast. She could be fun in the right circumstances—she'd come to a couple of Pelham Lane parties back in the days when she and Fitz were an item—but Tommi had never paid that much attention to her.

Hannah patted Flame, who nuzzled at her curiously. "Good boy," she crooned. "Ready to go win your very first blue ribbon?"

Marissa and Dani wandered over as Hannah, Flame, Elliot, and Fitz hurried off in the direction of the rings. "What's going on?" Dani asked. "Isn't that that eq girl from Kara Parodi's barn?"

"Yeah, I was just about to tell you." Marissa smirked. "Guess who's back with Fitz?"

"No!" Dani's eyes widened. "Are you serious? What about Kate?"

Tommi didn't stick around to hear any more. She hurried after Flame and his entourage, catching up as they reached the warm-up ring. It was crowded with riders getting ready for the under-eighteen flat eq class that had just started in a nearby ring. Could Fitz have entered Flame in that? He gave Hannah a leg up into the saddle, then opened the gate to let her in.

"Take it easy out there," he instructed as Hannah fiddled with her stirrups. "Flame doesn't have much experience with crowded warm-up rings."

"Got it." Hannah picked up the reins, steering the horse into a walk near the center as the faster-moving horses cantered by on the rail. Fitz spotted Tommi watching and came over to join her at the fence.

"He's looking good, huh?" Fitz commented.

"Sure, Kate's done good work training him so far." Tommi shot him a look. "So is Jamie coming to warm them up, or what?"

Fitz shrugged. "He said he'd be here if he finishes at the jumper ring in time."

Tommi narrowed her eyes. Before she could ask any more questions, Marissa and Dani hurried over. "So Hyper Hannah's riding your horse now, huh?" Marissa said to Fitz.

"Ssh." Fitz flapped his hand at them. "Gossip later, okay? I need to pay attention."

They all kept quiet and watched the warm-up. Hannah looked tense from the start, and it was obvious that Flame was picking up on it. Tommi could see that he was trying to be good, but within moments his long, flowing stride got quick and short and his nostrils were flaring nervously. Every time a horse passed him at a gait faster than a walk, he spun and tried to follow it.

"Yikes," Marissa murmured as Hannah circled Flame right in front of another horse, almost causing a crash. A trainer standing nearby cursed loudly, though Hannah barely seemed aware of it.

"She really needs to relax—she's freaking him out," Tommi said.

Fitz frowned. "She's still getting used to him. This is only her second time on him, you know."

"Okay. But that's what a catch rider does, right?" Tommi flicked her eyes toward him. "She gets on and gets the job done, even if she's never set eyes on the horse before." She couldn't resist adding, "I've seen Kate do it a million times."

"Ooh, burn!" Dani whispered, stifling a giggle when Fitz shot her a sour look.

Tommi turned to watch again. Flame was fighting Hannah's rigid hands by twisting his neck and shaking his head. He was so counterbent that he almost ran into another passing horse.

"This obviously isn't working," Tommi said, wincing as Flame spooked at yet another horse coming toward him. "They're not ready."

Marissa and Dani nodded, but Fitz didn't comment. They all watched Hannah kick Flame into a canter.

"Uh-oh," Dani murmured as Flame leaped into a near-gallop.

Tommi held her breath, almost afraid to watch. Hannah pulled back on the reins, but Flame tossed his head and sped up, his ears pricked toward a couple of bays loping along in front of him.

"Whoa, whoa!" Hannah shouted. She cranked the horse's head to one side.

"Yikes!" Marissa exclaimed as one of the bays veered out into Flame's path. Luckily Flame managed to dodge around it, though Hannah let out a squeak and grabbed mane as she lost a stirrup. Flame didn't seem to notice; as soon as he'd passed the bays, he lunged after another horse trotting farther ahead, his stride lengthening and his ears back.

"Wow," Dani commented. "And I thought *Red* had track flashbacks!"

"Seriously." Marissa gasped as Hannah teetered in the saddle. Somehow, though, the girl managed to recover, shoving her foot back into the stirrup and gathering up her reins with a grim look on her face. She managed to slow Flame to a rough trot, though he kept snorting and staring around at the other horses.

"Sorry I'm late. How's it going?"

Tommi glanced over her shoulder. Jamie had arrived. Thank God.

The trainer glanced out at the ring, his keen blue eyes immediately fixing on Flame and his rider. A second later he was striding into the ring to put a stop to the ride. Fitz tried to protest, and Hannah cried a little, but Jamie didn't pay attention to any of that, insisting they scratch from the class.

"You can try again in the open flat eq tomorrow if you want," the trainer said, though it was obvious—to Tommi at least—that he didn't think that was a good idea, either. "But today's not happening."

Fitz scowled. "Fine," he snapped. "Trainer knows best, right?" He spun away, putting an arm around Hannah, who had dismounted by now. She burst into fresh tears.

"He just wouldn't listen to me!" she wailed as Fitz steered her away.

Jamie gave Flame a pat. "You okay cooling him out?" he asked Elliot, who was running up the stirrups. "I should try to catch the hack in ring three."

"Sure, boss," Elliot said.

"Wow," Dani said, watching as the groom led the horse toward the barns and Jamie disappeared in the opposite direction. "That was—exciting."

Tommi sighed. "Yeah."

EIGHTEEN

— — — — —

"Kate. I need to talk to you."

Kate froze, then turned slowly to face Fitz. She was so intent on what she was doing—fixing a couple of trashed braids on a restless pony—that she hadn't heard him coming.

"Y-yes?" she said cautiously.

He looked great, as always. He was ready to step into the show ring from the waist down in breeches and boots, though his shirt was unbuttoned at the top and his tie nowhere in sight. All perfectly normal for a show day. What wasn't normal was his face. His eyes were serious, and his mouth turned down at the corners.

"I'm sure Tommi or someone told you what happened when Hannah tried to show Flame yesterday," he said, his tone cool and weirdly formal. "It didn't go too well."

Kate shrugged. "Yeah, I heard."

Tommi had told her all about it, of course. Plus, according to Marissa, the incident had already made that new blog everyone was buzzing about lately. Not that Kate had time to read blogs, even ones about horse showing.

"Anyway," Fitz went on, "I'd still like to get Flame in the ring. I was hoping you could take him in open eq on the flat this afternoon."

The pony kicked at a fly and then stepped forward, straining against the cross-ties. Kate moved it back into place, using that as an excuse to avoid answering Fitz for a moment. Her first instinct was to say no to his request. She was tired of Fitz's games; tired of the way he was making her feel.

At the same time, she couldn't help remembering how *Flame* made her feel. Riding him. Helping him learn new things. Just spending time with him. How could she give that up?

Besides, if Hannah's ride had been half as bad as Tommi had made it sound, the poor horse had to be terribly confused. Didn't Kate owe it to him to fix that if she could, give him a good experience to replace the bad one? After all, she was the whole reason he was here in the first place.

"Sure," she blurted out before she could overthink it. "Um, I mean, that's fine. I just need to check with Jamie that I can fit it in around the classes he wants me to do today."

Fitz nodded. "I'll go ask him right now."

He spun on his heel and hurried off without another word. Kate bit the inside of her cheek and stared after him, feeling confused and angry and sad all at the same time. Then the pony shifted its weight again, and Kate did her best to forget about Fitz as she went back to work.

"Oh, is this really the place? It's simply gorgeous!" Gina exclaimed. "Reminds me of an estate in Connecticut where I filmed a TV guest spot once."

Zara glanced at the big stone mansion perched on the hill overlooking the busy showgrounds. "Yeah, it's a postcard." She pointed to a hand-lettered sign tacked to a fencepost. "Looks like we're supposed to park over there."

Her mother steered the Mercedes that way, driving slowly due to the uneven ground. Zillion-dollar estate, and they couldn't even afford a little gravel for the roads? Lame. But Zara wasn't going to worry about it. After being stuck in her stupid apartment all week, she was glad to be out in civilization again. Or whatever this was, anyway.

She glanced over her shoulder at Stacie, who was slumped in the backseat staring blankly out the window. The girl had spent the past two days bursting into tears every few minutes over that loser who'd dumped her. Thank God Zara had come up with that story about her old-fogey friend dying, or Gina would've known something was up for sure.

In any case, Zara couldn't help an evil little flash of amusement when she noticed the bored look on her cousin's face. Served her right. After the way she'd ditched Zara with no warning, the least Stacie could do was come to the show and play good girl for the weekend.

"Hey, wait," Zara said as they passed the edge of the stabling area. A couple of rigs were idling there as grooms unloaded horses from the trailers. "Stop here and drop me off. Then you two can go park, okay?"

"Of course, love." Gina stopped the car, then reached over and squeezed Zara's arm. "Break a leg."

Zara rolled her eyes. "Okay, I know that's an acting thing," she joked. "But maybe not the best thing to say to a rider."

"Oops!" Gina laughed as if it was the funniest thing she'd ever heard, though Stacie didn't even crack a smile. Good.

"Bye-bye, Cousin Stacie," Zara said sweetly. "Hope you have fun watching the show!"

Pelham Lane's stalls were easy to find, since they were in the tent closest to the main ring. Right in the center of things, as always. Jamie didn't mess around.

Inside, Zara found Summer holding court in the tack stall, sitting on one of the director's chairs and blabbing about her party to Tommi, Marissa, and Dani. Of the three, only Marissa was even pretending to look interested. Dani was playing with her cell phone, and Tommi was fussing around with her spurs.

"Hi, people." Zara stepped inside. "I'm here."

"Zara!" Marissa turned to grin at her. "You've been holding out on us! Summer says you're bringing some hot older guy as your date tonight."

"Yeah, I heard it even made that new horse-showing blog." Dani smirked and waggled her eyebrows. "So spill, girl—who is he? Anyone we've heard of? Some heartthrobby young actor friend of your mom's, maybe?"

Zara shot Summer an annoyed look. Why had she told her about Marcus? Call it temporary insanity. And bad timing. He'd called to tell Zara he was coming to the party, and when the phone rang again a minute later Zara had assumed it was him calling back.

But no. It was Summer. And telling her about Marcus was

better than listening to her whine about her stupid ears again. At least, it had seemed that way at the time.

"You guys will just have to wait and see," Summer broke in, seeming peeved that the attention had shifted away from her. "But listen, I didn't finish telling you about the dessert cart—"

Just then Kate stuck her head into the tack stall. "Marissa," she said. "Miguel is looking for you. Miles is almost ready for your warm-up, but Miguel needs to know if you want to use your old saddle or the new one."

"Oops! I didn't realize it was so late." Marissa checked her watch. "I'd better go find my crop and helmet."

"I'll help you." Dani swung herself onto her crutches and hurried out of the room after her friend.

Meanwhile Tommi was heading for the door, too. "Hey Kate!" she called out. "Hold up a sec."

Soon they were all gone, leaving Zara alone with Summer. "Hey," Zara said with a little frown. "What's the big idea, blabbing my love life all over the barn?"

Summer shrugged, picking at her fingernails. "I hope I have time to get a manicure while they're doing my hair this afternoon," she said. Then, belatedly realizing that Zara had said something, she glanced up. "Wait, what?"

Zara grabbed a handful of peanuts out of the silver bowl on the tack trunk. "You," she said, crunching the salty nuts. "Telling everyone about my new guy."

"So what?" Summer said. "Everyone's going to see him at the party tonight anyway."

"So not the point. How would you like it if I went around

blabbing stuff about you? Maybe revealing certain things you don't want anyone to know on that HorseShowSecrets blog?" She stuck her fingers behind her ears, pushing them forward so they stuck straight out from her head.

Summer's face fell. "No!" she whispered, her blue eyes panicky as they darted around the room, making sure nobody was nearby. "Please, Zara. You can't tell anyone about that! Especially right before my big night! I'd die!" She stood up, her eyes filling with tears. "I'd totally die!"

She rushed out of the tack stall. "Summer, wait!" Zara called.

But it was too late. She was gone. Zara didn't usually feel much sympathy for Summer. But this time, she couldn't help feeling a little guilty. She'd seemed *really* upset.

And it wasn't as if Zara would actually give away someone's deep dark secrets on some stupid blog. She wasn't like that. Summer had to know that, right?

She pulled out her phone, logging onto the Internet as she wandered out into the aisle. Tommi and Kate were just outside, huddled close together, deep in conversation. They broke apart when they saw Zara coming.

"Are you okay?" Tommi asked.

Zara glanced up at her and grimaced. "Just checking out the latest news about myself on HorseShowSecrets," she said. "I just *love* having everyone on the Internet know my business, don't you?"

"HorseShowSecrets?" Tommi shrugged. "Yeah, I've been hearing people talk about that all week. It's some kind of blog or something?"

"Yeah. Check it out." Zara had just pulled up the blog on her phone. She scrolled down until she spotted the most recent entry with her name in it. It was short, basically just a couple of lines, speculating about Zara's "tall, dark, and mysterious" new guy.

Zara scowled as she read it. The only people she'd told about Marcus coming to tonight's party were Summer, Gina, and Stacie. And she was pretty sure her mother didn't have anything to do with this. Gina might be a publicity hound when it came to her own career, but she and Zac both did their best to keep Zara's name out of the papers whenever possible.

"Let me see." Tommi reached for Zara's phone.

Zara handed it over, still trying to figure out who'd blabbed. Cousin Stacie? Not a likely suspect either. Zara had barely let the girl out of her sight since her return. No sense taking any chances of Stacie blurting out something incriminating in front of Gina.

So that left Summer. Could she be writing the blog to drum up publicity for her stupid party? Fury coursed through Zara's veins; that had to be it! She clenched her fists, ready to find Summer and string her up by her stupid pinned-back ears.

"I can't believe this," Tommi commented, breaking into Zara's thoughts. She was frowning as she scrolled through the site. "Who would even know some of this stuff? Could it be someone right here at—"

She cut herself off, staring at the tiny screen.

"What?" Kate asked.

"There's . . ." Tommi hesitated, glancing at Kate and then back at the phone. "There's an entry about you."

"Really?" Kate said.

Zara was surprised, too. Kate wasn't exactly gossip fodder, unless you counted barn work as thrilling news. "What's it say?"

Tommi bit her lip. "Just that, um, Kate and Fitz broke up."

"Whoa! Really?" Zara shot a look at Kate. For the first time, she noticed that the girl looked kind of upset. "Bummer. But hey, there's other fish in the sea, right?"

Kate didn't answer. Tommi was still scanning the blog, looking annoyed. "It's got to be someone with an in at Pelham Lane."

"Yeah. Specifically, Summer." Zara felt her own annoyance bubbling up again. "She's the only one I told about my date to her ridiculous party."

Tommi looked thoughtful. "Summer? Doubtful. The girl has the attention span of a gnat. No way would she actually keep up with a blog like this. Anyway, all she had to do was mention what you told her to someone else. Like Marissa, for instance. The girl's a gossip freak. If she found out, it'd be all over the circuit in about ten seconds flat. No blog required."

"Do you think Marissa's the one behind HorseShow-Secrets?" Kate asked.

Whatever Tommi said next, Zara didn't hear it. Something had just occurred to her. There was one more person who knew about her date with Marcus tonight.

Marcus himself.

Her heart started pounding as she quickly put two and two together. Marcus wouldn't tell her much about his past. He was practically pathological about changing the subject back to her, now that she thought about it. But one of the only things he'd said was that he used to ride. Could he actually be a rider from another barn? Could *he* be the one writing HorseShowSecrets?

Suddenly it all made perfect sense. Especially when she remembered that snarky little entry about Ellie being too hot for her to handle. Hadn't that appeared right after she'd joked around with Marcus about Ellie being hyper and bucking her off?

"That bastard!" she hissed.

"Huh?" Tommi said as she and Kate turned to stare.

But Zara didn't bother to stop and explain. She was fuming. She should have known Marcus was too good to be true!

"Give me that," she said, snatching her phone out of Tommi's hand. "I need to make a very important call."

NINETEEN

— — — — —

"What was that all about?" Tommi wondered aloud as she watched Zara stomp off down the aisle.

She glanced at Kate, who looked as beaten down as a kicked puppy. Tommi's anger flared when she thought about how Fitz was acting, though she wasn't sure what to do about it. It *would* be satisfying to find him and punch him in the neck. But that wouldn't do anyone much good, especially Kate.

"So anyway, where were we?" she said. "Are you really going to ride Flame later?"

Kate shrugged, picking at a cuticle. "I said I would. And Jamie says it's okay." Finally she looked up. "You should probably start getting Legs warmed up for your jumper class. Need any help?"

"It's okay, I've got it." Tommi hesitated, hating the sad look in Kate's eyes, trying to come up with the magic words that would make everything all better.

Then she heard someone calling her name. Glancing that way, she saw Alex hurrying toward them.

"I made it!" he called out with a grin. "Man, this place is out in the middle of nowhere, isn't it?"

"Hi." Tommi tilted her head back as he bent down to kiss her. "You remember Kate, right?"

"Sure. Hi." Alex smiled at Kate, raking one hand through his spiky dark hair. "You showing at this thing too?"

"Uh-huh." Kate flashed a brief smile. "Actually, I should go. I need to start tacking up for the pre-greens soon, and I've got stuff to finish before then."

She hurried away. Tommi chewed her lip, watching her go. Alex was talking again, chattering about the traffic or something, but she barely heard him.

She tuned back in when he slipped his arm around her waist. "So what time does the party start, anyway?" he asked. "We have time to grab some dinner beforehand? I saw this fun-looking little Mexican place on my way here."

"What?" Tommi glanced at her watch. Kate was right; she needed to get on Legs about five minutes ago to be ready for their next class. "Um, I think they're serving dinner at the party. But listen, I should go see if my horse is tacked up yet."

He grinned, giving her a squeeze. "I thought you paid all those fancy grooms to worry about stuff like that," he said. "Seriously, though, I was hoping we could hang out. Sure you can't play hooky for a little while?"

"I'm sure. Sorry." Tommi tried to keep her voice and expression pleasant. For some reason, it wasn't easy. Alex had just arrived, but he was already rubbing her the wrong way.

But that wasn't his fault, right? She was just stressed because she was running late.

Meanwhile he let go of her and stepped away to peek into

the tack stall. "Nice setup," he commented. "Is that where you guys hang out? How come nobody's in there right now?"

"Because everyone's busy showing or getting ready to." Tommi shot him a tight smile, hoping he'd finally take the hint before she had to hit him over the head with it. "Including me. You can tag along if you want, but I really need to go find my horse now."

"Okay." He fell into step as she started down the aisle toward Legs's stall. "Hey, so how many people are going to this party tonight, anyway? Is Zara going to be there?"

Tommi stopped short, her impatience bubbling over into actual irritation. This was too much for her to deal with right now. In fact, it suddenly felt like too much to deal with *ever*.

She turned to face him. "As a matter of fact, yes she is," she said evenly. "And you're totally welcome to hang out with her if you want. Because I'm starting to think maybe that's who you really ought to be with."

"What?" Alex looked startled, then slightly guilty. "No! That's not true. I just like to talk to her about her dad, you know—"

"Yeah," Tommi cut him off. She so didn't have time for this scene. "I know. Listen, Alex. You're a great guy, and we've had some fun together. I used to think we had a lot in common, but lately I'm thinking maybe we don't. And, well, basically it's just not working for me, okay? Sorry. You can still go to the party if you want, though."

Alex opened his mouth, then closed it again. "Wait," he said. "Are you dumping me?"

Tommi shrugged; she'd just spotted Javier coming toward

her leading Legs, who was all tacked up for their jumper class. "Sorry," she said again, trying not to notice the hurt and confusion in his eyes as she rushed off toward her horse.

Zara felt a little better as soon as she'd sent a text to Marcus telling him not to bother coming tonight after all. There. That should show him she wasn't the sucker he thought she was. Good thing she'd figured out what kind of person he really was before it was too late.

A moment later her phone rang. She glanced at the screen.

"What do you want?" she spat into the mouthpiece. "I told you, I don't want to see you."

"Zara?" Marcus sounded confused. And maybe a little annoyed. "What's going on? I got your text."

"Yeah, that's kind of why I sent it." Zara rolled her eyes.

"Listen, if this is some kind of joke, I don't get it." He sounded even more annoyed now. "I took off work to go to your party, and I'm halfway to Trenton on the train right now."

The train? That threw Zara off for a split second. Who took the train?

But she shook it off; that wasn't really the point. "You can stop the Mr. Innocent act," she said. "I know why you've been hanging out with me. I saw your pathetic little blog."

"Blog? What blog?"

"Duh! Are you going to make me spell it out?" She clutched the phone harder. "HorseShowSecrets! I know you've got to have something to do with it. Are you writing it yourself, or just feeding dirt about me to whoever is?"

He was silent for a second or two. "Hold on," he said at last. "You think I wrote gossip about you on some blog? What the hell kind of person do you think I am?"

"The kind who does crap like that, obviously." Zara couldn't believe he was still trying to BS his way out of this. "I thought you were different. But you're just another vulture, waiting around to flatter the stupid little celeb-u-chick into giving you what you want, right?"

He was silent again, for longer this time. "I see," he said slowly. "Okay, so you think I really just hung out with you because your parents are celebrities?"

"I don't just think it. I *know* it."

"Great." His voice was cold. "Then this obviously isn't going to work out. Good thing I found that out before I wasted any more time."

"Before *you* wasted—" Zara began hotly.

He didn't let her finish. "Looks like I'll be switching trains at the next stop and heading back to the city," he said. "Have a nice life, Zara."

Click.

Zara frowned, lowering the phone and staring at it. That hadn't gone quite the way she'd expected. Most of those paparazzi types at least tried to talk their way out of trouble when they got caught scamming someone. Zara knew that from personal experience.

Then again, Marcus hadn't seemed like the usual type. In more ways than one . . .

"Steady, big guy," Tommi murmured as Legs spurted forward at the lightest touch of her leg. They'd just entered the show ring, and the lanky bay gelding was pricking his ears at the colorful jumps.

Tommi took him around in a big, loopy circle, letting him take a peek at a few of the spookiest obstacles as they cantered past. Their warm-up had started off a little rough; Tommi was distracted, and Legs could tell. But when the horse had almost stopped at the first warm-up jump, she'd forced her mind back to business, channeling her emotions into focus and determination. Now, as she ran through the course in her mind, she felt ready.

"Let's go," she whispered as she turned the horse toward the timers.

Legs pricked his ears at the first jump. He surged forward eagerly when Tommi asked him to, meeting the obstacle out of stride. They sailed over, and Tommi smiled.

Alex was the furthest thing from her mind as she and the horse hunted the next jump, clearing it just as effortlessly as the first. The course was a challenging one with lots of twists and turns, but that was just what Legs liked. Anytime he started to get strong or distracted, there was another rollback or tricky distance to grab his attention.

By the end of the round, Tommi was grinning. "Good boy!" she exclaimed, giving him a big pat as they passed through the timers again. They'd gone clear and fast; it was probably one of their best rounds ever.

She was still smiling as she rode out of the ring. Jamie hurried toward her.

"Nice," he said. "Way to show them how it's done."

"Thanks." Tommi heard cheering from nearby. Glancing over, she waved to the little group of railbirds from Pelham Lane over at the fence near the gate—Dani, Marissa, a couple of adult riders.

Miguel appeared at the horse's head. "Good round," he said. "Want me to cool him out for you?"

"It's okay, I can do it," Tommi told him with a smile.

As she dismounted, she saw someone pushing toward her through the crowd. It was Kara Parodi, a big-name trainer who ran one of the most successful barns in New Jersey.

"Tommi," the woman said in her brisk, no-nonsense voice. "Is that horse of yours still for sale?"

Tommi swallowed hard, remembering that Kara had been interested in looking at Legs for a client of hers at a show a few weeks ago. Unfortunately, it hadn't worked out that day, and Tommi hadn't heard from her again. Until now.

"Yes," she said. "As a matter of fact, he is."

"Good." Kara nodded. "I want to ask you a few questions about him. You got a minute?"

"Sure." Tommi glanced at Miguel, who was still holding Legs by the reins. "Hey, Miguel—" she began.

"I've got it." The groom winked, then led the horse away.

Tommi took a deep breath, wiped her suddenly sweaty palms on her breeches, and turned to face the trainer. "Okay, what did you want to ask me?"

Kate's legs closed softly against Flame's sides as the ringmaster called for a trot. Flame responded instantly, settling into his typical steady rhythm, though his body was tenser than usual. Kate felt him twitch as a huge warmblood thundered past them on the inside. She bent Flame slightly to the outside. That brought his attention back to her long enough for him to forget about the other horse. Good. Those lateral exercises they'd practiced were paying off. So was their long warm-up session.

She half-halted lightly, steadying the horse's stride as his ears flicked back, listening to the horses behind him. He let out a sigh and relaxed. The eq class was more than half over, and it was going well. *Really* well. Almost kind of magical, all things considered.

"Canter, please," the ringmaster said. "All canter."

"Easy," Kate breathed as she touched her outside heel to her horse's side and he stepped into a canter. She felt an extra surge of energy run through him, but held with her seat until he settled.

She wanted to hold her breath as they cantered softly around the corner. Instead she timed her breaths to the rhythm of his canter. One, two, three, one, two, three . . .

As the ringmaster brought them back to a walk and asked the class to line up, Kate felt a grin split her face from ear to ear. She was so proud of the horse that she was ready to burst. Who cared if he was a few weeks off the tracks or a few months? That had been an impressive performance for any green horse. *Especially* one that had barely been in a ring with other horses before.

"Good boy," she whispered under her breath as she waited for the results. "Good, good boy!"

It wasn't until she heard cheers and hollers—including

Dani's familiar whoop—that she noticed the announcer repeating her name.

"Nice job," the ringmaster said with a smile as she pinned a blue ribbon onto Flame's bridle. Flame tilted his head and stuck out his tongue, trying to catch the shiny fabric flapping from his face, and Kate laughed.

"Thanks," she said to the ringmaster as she rubbed Flame's withers. Sure, an equitation class was judged solely on the rider. But Kate couldn't have done her part without a willing partner. And Flame had just showed that he was more than willing to put that bad experience with Hannah behind him and step up. She was so proud of him she could hardly stand it.

When she rode toward the gate, she saw that it wasn't just people from her own barn cheering them on. Almost everyone at the rail was joining in, including a couple of trainers she recognized from other barns. She felt her cheeks go pink, and bent forward to pat the horse as the ring steward swung the gate open.

"Kate, that was incredible!" Jamie exclaimed, giving Flame a sound pat on the neck. "Well done!"

"I know! Wasn't he great?" Kate said breathlessly. She slid down from the saddle and threw her arms around Jamie. He wasn't normally a huggy type of trainer, but this time he just laughed and squeezed her back.

Behind him, Marissa was jumping up and down and squealing. "I knew you were going to win that class!"

"I know, right?" Dani exclaimed. "Flame looked like a whole different horse than that hot mess he was yesterday!"

Kate grinned at them, then spun around to see if Tommi

was there. Instead she saw Fitz coming toward her. "You two were amazing!" he blurted out, his eyes sparkling and a big grin on his face. "That horse was *born* to show!"

He flung his arms around her. Kate hugged him back, still too excited to realize what was happening.

Then she stiffened, remembering. She pulled back.

Fitz seemed to catch on at the same moment. He let her go, rubbing his head and swallowing hard as his smile faded. Their eyes met.

"Kate . . . ," he began uncertainly.

"Fitz!" someone squealed. Hannah pushed her way past Kate and flung herself at him. "Oh my God, you were right! That horse is going to be a superstar! Congratulations!"

Kate turned away, her heart plummeting into her feet. It felt as if all the excitement of the past few minutes had been sucked out of her, replaced by a sick feeling in the pit of her stomach.

"I'd better get him back to the barn," she said softly, reaching to take Flame's reins from Jamie. She led the horse away without looking back.

TWENTY

— — — — —

Kate tugged at her skirt. The dress she was wearing was at least two years old, and she'd grown an inch or more since then. But it was the only halfway decent dress she owned, and she couldn't afford to buy a new one just for Summer's party. Up until a couple of hours ago, she hadn't even been planning to attend. Why had she let Tommi talk her into coming?

Oh, right. Because Tommi was her friend, and she'd convinced Kate that she needed her. That they could have fun being newly single together.

"Wow!" someone said in Kate's ear. "This place is looking pretty swanky, huh?"

It was Dani. Marissa was with her. Both girls looked cute and stylish, which just made Kate feel more out of place than ever. Dani had decorated her crutches and cast with glossy satin ribbons that matched her cherry red dress. A digital camera dangled from her wrist, which Kate only noticed when Dani whipped it up and took a photo of her.

"Hey!" Kate blinked, spots dancing in front of her eyes from the flash. "Stop. I look terrible."

"You look adorable." Marissa giggled, sounding breathless and excited as she glanced around. "Crazy party, huh?"

The Sweet Sixteen party was taking place in something called the Grand Ballroom. And it *was* pretty grand. It was a cavernous room with columns holding up the high ceiling. The band was playing at one end of the room, and a few people were already dancing. A long row of French doors opened onto a flagstone patio, where more guests were chatting or admiring the view of the mansion's lawn and flower gardens, sweeping away into the lowering dusk.

"Can you believe that ice sculpture?" Marissa stared toward the buffet, looking amused. "Only Summer would insist on a life-size horse and rider!"

Dani peered at the ice sculpture, which was standing on a marble pedestal between two buffet tables. "Is that supposed to be Summer riding?" she asked with a smirk. "Because if it is, she really needs to work on her leg position."

Kate glanced at the door, wishing Tommi would get there already. She'd texted when Kate was walking up from the parking lot with Jamie and Elliot, saying that something had come up and she'd be a few minutes late.

There was a sudden clatter of hooves from the direction of the patio. "Come on, Summer told us about this part, remember?" Marissa sounded excited. "Let's go see her grand entrance!"

Kate trailed along after the two girls as they rushed out through the French doors. They all emerged just in time to see a ridiculously ornate carriage roll onto the flagstones. It was being pulled by a snow-white Percheron with a plume of pink feathers spouting from its browband.

"Woo-hoo, Cinderella!" Dani whooped, snapping several photos as Summer waved to the crowd and then climbed out of the carriage, assisted by an older man in a tuxedo. Whiskey was there too, snapping irritably at the pink satin dog vest someone had stuffed him into.

"Is that her date?" Kate blurted out in surprise.

"What? The dog?" Marissa joked.

Dani laughed, then glanced at the older man. "That's her dad playing Prince Charming," she said. "Summer didn't bring a date—she says there'll be too many hot guys here to limit herself to just one."

"Here's hoping she's right." Marissa licked her lips and glanced around. "That's why *we're* here stag, right, girls?"

Dani nodded. "Looks like Summer's getting mobbed by relatives and stuff. Come on, let's go back inside and check out the food. We can say our happy birthdays later."

As she entered the ballroom, Kate glanced over at the door again and finally saw Tommi coming in. She was grinning from ear to ear.

Tommi spotted Kate and the others and rushed toward them. "Guess what?" she called as soon as she was close enough to be heard over the music. "I think I just sold Legs!"

Tommi was floating on air as she accepted congratulations from Kate, Marissa, and Dani. She could hardly believe this was happening.

"So spill it!" Dani demanded. "Who bought him?"

"Well, it's not final just yet. He still has to pass the vetting." Tommi lifted her hand, showing that her fingers were crossed. "But Kara Parodi brought one of her clients to see him."

"Anyone we know?" Marissa asked, shooting a quick look toward Kate.

Tommi grimaced, remembering that Fitz's little friend Hannah was one of Kara's students. "Not a junior," she said quickly, hoping Kate hadn't noticed Marissa's look. "This was an adult jumper rider. She's in her late twenties and has been doing the level fives and looking to move up. She's pretty brave and athletic."

"That sounds perfect for Legs," Kate put in.

Tommi nodded. "They got along great. I think they'll be a fantastic team." She hugged herself, hardly daring to believe the way this had worked out. After all the false starts, the inappropriate buyers, the annoying calls and texts . . . But that stuff was water under the bridge now. It had all been worth it to get Legs into the perfect home.

She couldn't help a twinge of sadness that the horse would be leaving. But mostly she was relieved that she'd actually done it. She'd sold him, for close to her asking price and well before the deadline. Now her father would have to see that she really could make this work.

"I can't wait to tell my dad," she said. "But first I need to tell Jamie. Have you guys seen him?"

"I walked up with him, but I haven't seen him since." Kate glanced around. "This place is getting more crowded by the—eep!"

Her eyes had just gone wide and nervous as she stared over toward the dance floor. Tommi followed her gaze and realized what she'd just seen. Alex. With Zara. The band had just started an up-tempo song, and the two of them were dancing. Very close together.

"Oh," Tommi said. "Yeah. I thought that might happen."

Marissa and Dani were looking that way by now, too. "Okay, what's up with that?" Marissa asked. "I thought Zara had her own date; why's she stealing yours?"

"He's not mine." Tommi kept her voice neutral. "Alex is a free agent; we broke up."

"Oh?" Dani sounded curious, but Tommi didn't feel like explaining just then. She watched out of the corner of her eye as Alex grabbed Zara and twirled her around.

Tommi felt a tiny pang of something—jealousy? Regret? Annoyance? She wasn't quite sure.

Whatever it was, she tried to tamp it down before it could ruin her good mood. After all, *she* was the one who'd broken things off. After watching Alex DJ that time, she just hadn't been able to look at him quite the same way. Then there was the way he seemed to be glomming onto Zara already, even though he knew she and Tommi were friends. Not exactly the coolest.

Still, the two of them had had some fun times together. And nobody was perfect, including her. One of her biggest imperfections? Being too impatient, too quick to cut her losses. Especially when it came to her boyfriends. Had she given up on Alex too fast?

To distract herself from such thoughts, she pulled her

phone out of her purse. "Guess I'll text Jamie and see where he is," she told the other girls. "Otherwise I'll never find him in this crowd."

She'd turned off the phone while Kara and her student were trying Legs, not wanting any interruptions. After that she'd been in such a hurry to rush back to the hotel and get changed that she'd forgotten to turn it back on again. She did so now and saw that she had a few new texts.

Most were ignorable, but one caught her eye. It was from Gabe, the nerdy but sweet guy she'd met at Penn, telling her about an upcoming lecture at the museum "in case you happen to be in town."

She smiled, flashing back to last weekend. It had been fun to play college student for a while. Maybe that kind of life wasn't for her, but then again, it was a lot easier now to imagine doing it for real. Only if she changed her mind about the horse thing, of course—and after today, she had no intention of doing that. Still, it was kind of nice to know that she had options.

Just then the band started another song. "Ooh, I like this one!" Dani started dancing in place, swaying back and forth on her crutches. "Come on, guys, let's dance!"

"Coming." Tommi typed out a quick text to Jamie, then followed the other girls onto the dance floor.

"You're a really good dancer," Alex said as the current song ended.

"Thanks." Zara shot him a look. She still couldn't believe

Tommi had dumped him right before this party. And that he'd showed up anyway. Or actually, maybe she could. He was already on her nerves after just one dance. "Think they're carding at this place?"

Alex grinned. "One way to find out. I'll be right back."

He disappeared into the crowd near the bar. Zara drifted over to a column and leaned against it, watching people dance. She noticed Summer hurrying past, peering down at the cell phone she was holding in both hands.

"Yo, birthday girl!" Zara called out. "How's it feel to be a year older?"

"Zara!" Summer looked up, then hurried over. Her face was flushed, making her look almost pretty. "Are you having a good time? Where's your mysterious date?"

Zara shrugged, not wanting to get into it. Thinking about Marcus made her feel cranky. "He couldn't make it after all."

"Oh." That seemed to throw Summer off for a second. She glanced around, then leaned closer. "Listen, thanks for not telling anyone about—you know. Before my party, at least."

Zara was about to roll her eyes. Then Summer shot another nervous look around the room and smoothed down her hair, which fell in soft blond waves over her ears.

Suddenly Zara's snarky feelings faded away. Yeah, Summer was super annoying and shallow. But she obviously wasn't quite as secure and self-confident as she wanted everyone to believe. Then again, who was?

"Chill out," Zara told her. "I'm not going to tell anyone about that. Ever, okay?"

Summer met her eye, her expression uncertain. "Really?"

"Cross my heart." Zara drew a big X over her own chest. "No matter what you read on the blogs, you can trust me."

Summer smiled, though Zara thought she still saw a hint of doubt behind it. "Thanks, Zara. You're a good friend." Suddenly Summer's eyes lit up as she glanced at the phone in her hand. "OMG, I almost forgot," she exclaimed, sounding more like her usual giddy self. "Speaking of the blog, check this out!"

She shoved the phone at Zara. The HorseShowSecrets blog was on the screen.

"Seriously?" This time Zara did roll her eyes. "If you have time to check the Internet, you obviously need someone to teach you how to party."

"No, look!" Summer was hopping up and down like a little kid who had to pee. "Check out the latest entry. It's *about* this party!"

"What?" Zara took a closer look. Sure enough, the mystery blogger had posted something new just a few minutes ago. There was a brief blurb about the "party of the millennium," along with several photos showing the crowded ballroom, the band, even the ridiculous ice sculpture.

"Isn't that cool?" Summer said. "Whoever's doing the blog must be right here at the party!" She giggled. "Not that that narrows it down much if you're trying to guess who it is. Half the A circuit is here!"

"Yeah." Zara stared at the phone as the meaning of that sank in.

"Ooh!" Summer squeaked. "There's my aunt and cousin from Michigan. I should go say hi." She plucked the phone out of Zara's hand and took off toward the door.

Zara just stood there for a moment, too stunned to move. Because she'd just realized something. Summer was right— whoever was behind HorseShowSecrets must be at this party. That was the only way he or she could have posted those photos.

But that meant there was one person who *couldn't* be behind the blog. Or the photos. Or, most likely, all the stuff about Zara that had appeared earlier.

"Marcus," she whispered.

Her heart sank. Oh God. She'd just totally screwed things up with a really cool guy. Maybe the coolest guy she'd ever met.

"Hey!" Alex hurried over with two glasses in his hands. "Check it out, the guy barely even glanced at my fake ID. Hope you like gin and tonic."

"Yeah." Zara took the glass and gulped down about half the drink, savoring the feel of the alcohol burning her throat. "It's cool. I'm not hard to please."

Alex chugged part of his drink, too. His foot was tapping as the band played some lame-ass hit from earlier in the summer.

"This is a good tune," he said, glancing out at the dance floor. "Want to get back out there?"

Zara didn't really feel like dancing. Especially with Alex. Now that he and Tommi had broken up, she didn't have to be nice to him anymore, right?

"Nope," she said. "Thanks for the drink, though."

She hurried off and lost herself in the crowd before he could respond.

Kate sneaked a look at her watch. It was only a little after eight, but she was already tired. Morning came early on show days, and she had to get up and do it all again tomorrow.

She glanced at Tommi, who was standing nearby chatting with some people Kate vaguely recognized as junior riders from another big show barn. Tommi's face was flushed, and she was smiling almost nonstop. Kate was happy for her, even if she wasn't exactly in a party mood herself.

What was she still doing here, anyway? She didn't fit in, and it wasn't as if Summer would miss her if she left. Or Tommi, for that matter—she was in a good mood now and didn't really need her anymore.

Kate checked the time again, mentally calculating how many hours' sleep she could get if she left right now. When she looked up again, she froze. Fitz had just walked in.

He didn't see her yet; his eyes swept the room, settling on the platform where the band was playing a jazzy version of "Happy Birthday." Kate's heart thumped, and she shot a look at the door. If she made a run for it, she could escape before he even realized she was here.

"Fitz!" a high-pitched voice cried out with a giggle.

Kate turned her head and saw Hannah making a beeline for Fitz. He glanced at her, but barely paused to speak to her before continuing to weave his way through the crowd. Hannah stayed where she was, looking slightly confused.

Kate's eyes followed Fitz. She knew she should go. Why torture herself? But her body seemed to be as frozen in place as that ice sculpture over at the buffet.

Fitz stopped in front of the stage and gestured to the lead singer, who stepped forward and leaned toward him. The two of them spoke briefly, though Kate was too far away to hear anything they said.

A moment later Fitz stepped back and the singer took the microphone. "Ladies and gentlemen," he said, "we have a request." He glanced back at his bandmates. "Hit it, guys."

They launched into a different song. Kate was so distracted by watching Fitz that it took her a moment to recognize it.

"Oh, man," one of the girls over by Tommi said loudly, glancing toward the band. "Seriously, someone actually requested 'Forgive Me'? That song is so over!"

Kate hardly heard her. Fitz had just spotted her; his eyes locked on to hers as he walked toward her.

"Hey," he said softly when he reached her. For the first time, Kate noticed that he was holding a flower, a single perfect daisy. He held it out to her. "Here, I wanted to give you this. And to say I'm sorry."

"I—what?" Kate stammered.

His eyes were serious as he gazed into hers. "Yeah. No grand gesture this time," he said. "Just the honest truth. The thing is, I don't really know how to do this relationship thing, you know?"

Kate nodded, though she wasn't sure what he was talking about. Out of the corner of her eye she could see Tommi watching from nearby, a look of concern on her face. But Kate ignored her, staying focused on Fitz. Trying to figure out what he was saying.

Fitz sighed and ran his hand through his reddish-blond hair. "So when things got hard," he went on, "I wasn't sure what else to do but give up. Move on. Business as usual."

"Oh." Kate felt more confused than ever.

"Then you hugged me earlier—you know, after Flame totally ruled the eq ring." A ghost of his usual smile flitted across his face; a second later he went serious again. "And that's when I realized the truth. You've got a hold on me, Kate." He reached for her hand, swallowing hard. "Way more than any other girl I've ever met."

"R-really?" Kate glanced down at her hand, which looked small and pale clutched in his.

"I realized you're more than worth getting through the hard times." His voice was almost a whisper now. He took a step closer. "And the wait."

She blushed, flashing back to that night in his guest bedroom. But she quickly pushed that aside. She got what he was saying now. He wanted her forgiveness; wanted to get back together. Try again. But could she trust him, especially after he'd been so quick to move on?

"What about the other girls?" she blurted out, feeling her face go redder than ever. "You know, Hannah—"

"Yeah, I was an idiot." Fitz squeezed her hand. "Seriously, Hannah means nothing to me. I only hung out with her to make you jealous." His mouth twisted into a wry half smile. "Real mature, right? But I swear, nothing happened between us. Just, you know, the Flame stuff."

"Oh." Kate felt a stab of hope, then remembered something else. "And Sharon? What about her?"

"Sharon?" He looked confused for a second, then his face cleared and he laughed. "Oh my God, I almost forgot about that! Kate, Sharon lives in my building. She's like eighty, and she's a total Broadway freak." He shrugged, his eyes regaining some of their usual twinkle. "And yeah, I have to admit you've got me there. Sharon and I did have a really good time on our 'date' that night."

Kate didn't say anything for a second. What could she say? He'd put her through a lot these past few days, and she wasn't sure she was ready to get over it just like that. But the way her knees went all wobbly when he looked at her . . .

"*Forgive me,*" he sang softly along with the band. "*I know I done wrong. Forgive me, girl, 'cause I'm weak and you're strong . . .*" He stopped singing and shot her a hopeful smile. "What do you say, Kate? I'll do better from now on, I swear. No matter what my reputation says."

Kate hesitated, still not sure. "I don't know . . . ," she began.

"What do I have to do, beg?" He waggled his eyebrows. "Because you know I'll do it."

He dropped to his knees, wrapping both arms around her waist. "Fitz!" Kate hissed, blushing again. "Stop!"

"Please, Kate!" he wailed loudly. "You have to forgive me! *Pleeeease!*"

Kate glanced around sheepishly. Tommi was still watching, and now she wasn't the only one. People were turning to stare, giggling and pointing. How many of the girls watching them right now had Fitz been with in the past? Did it matter?

Fitz threw his head back. "Waaaah!" he cried. "I'm soooooo lonely!"

More people were laughing by now. This time Kate couldn't help joining in. Who cared about the past? He was here right now, wanting—actually *begging*—to be with *her*. Wasn't that what really mattered?

"Fine, I forgive you," she said, tugging on his hair. "Just get up and stop making a fool of yourself, okay?"

He grinned, hopped to his feet, and stared at her hopefully. "Does that mean you'll give me another shot?"

This time she only hesitated for a split second. "Yeah," she said. "I'll give you one more chance if you give me one."

"Deal." He pulled her toward him.

Kate felt her whole body relax into his kiss. She didn't pull away even when she heard a few cheers and someone— Zara?—called out "Get a room!"

They only came up for air when the band started a new song, a popular current dance hit. People started streaming toward the dance floor.

"Shall we?" Fitz took her hand.

She smiled and nodded, and they ran out to join their friends. Tommi was dancing with Dani and Marissa and some other people. When she saw Kate coming, Tommi leaned toward her.

"You okay?" she whispered in Kate's ear.

Kate glanced at her and smiled. "Yeah," she replied. "More than okay, actually."

She let out a little shriek of surprise as Fitz grabbed her and spun her around into his arms. Then she laughed and stood on tiptoes to kiss him again, suddenly so overwhelmed with warmth, relief, and joy that she hoped this night would never end.

ACKNOWLEDGMENTS

I would like to acknowledge all my teachers at New York University who were supportive of my riding career. I never had to pick between school and riding, and I was able to take classes that would help me become the person I chose, not who anyone else wished to mold me into. As someone who never wanted to go to college, you taught me that learning can be something to embrace and have fun with, not to rebel against. Thank you for trusting me and believing in my dreams and me.

I have to give a special thank-you to Steve Hutkins, who also gave me the freedom to become the person I am today. Without your confidence in my career and me, I never would have seen graduation day, let alone come away from college with such an amazing experience. Thank you for letting me find myself.

Christian Oh

GEORGINA BLOOMBERG is the younger daughter of New
York City mayor Michael Bloomberg. An accomplished equestrian, Georgina is on the board of directors of the Equestrian
Aid Foundation, the United States Equestrian Federation, the
Hampton Classic Horse Show, and both the Bloomberg Family
and Bloomberg Sisters foundations. She is an Equine Welfare
Ambassador for the ASPCA and a member of Friends of Finn
for the Humane Society of the United States, as well as the
chairwoman of the HSUS Horse Council. In 2006, she founded
the charity The Rider's Closet, which collects used riding
clothes for those who are unable to afford them. Now run by
Pegasus Therapeutic Riding, the program has enabled thou-
sands of riders to stay in the sport and have the proper apparel
and equipment. She is a graduate of New York University's
Gallatin School of Individualized Study.

Georgina is donating a portion of her proceeds from this book
to Friends of Finn.

CATHERINE HAPKA has published many books for children and young adults, including several about horses. A lifelong horse lover, she rides several times per week and keeps three horses on her small farm in Chester County, Pennsylvania. In addition to writing and riding, she enjoys animals of all kinds, reading, gardening, music, and travel.

Find out what's next for
Tommi, Kate, and Zara in

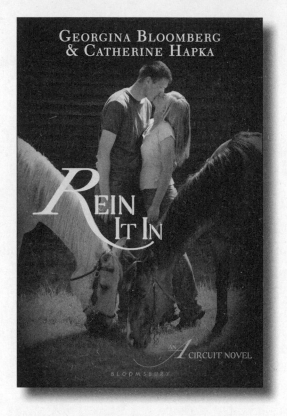

Only the best of the best qualify for an exclusive series of fall horse shows. And, of course, Tommi, Kate, and Zara are the best. Still, it's not exactly convenient that this show series starts up just as school is back in session. Can they handle the pressure of elite competition *and* high school?